Evernight Publishing

www.evernightpublishing.com

THE SUCCUBUS CHRONICLES

DEDICATION

To my favorite trickster—Owa'a Teygu'u Siyam

THE SUCCUBUS CHRONICLES

SOUL OF THE SUCCUBUS

Lila Shaw

Copyright © 2012

Chapter One

I slip out of the men's dressing room of Macy's—nourished but sick, sated but empty from what I hope will be the last nameless tryst of my existence. My life has been an endless loop of quick fucks and clandestine hookups. I live for and because of them. But I hate it, hate being a succubus.

For millennia I have existed as a sexual parasite upon humanity. I take men inside my body, coax out their essence and thrive. I feel nothing for them other than a fleeting spark of gratitude at best, contempt at worst. I'm tired of it, all of it. No price is too high to shed the curse.

Now, I seek the one who owns me, to demand my freedom. I've fulfilled my part of the bargain—one million souls delivered. Tonight I travel to Hell and I'll either return a free woman or I'll be destroyed.

Not many realize one of seven portals to Hell lies inside the meat locker of Gold's Texas Barbeque. The Golds know, of course, because it was part of Sol's contract with the devil.

I enter the sparsely populated restaurant and butcher shop between the lunch and dinner crowds. A cacophony of jingle bells on the door announces my arrival. Sol Gold shuffles out to assist me.

"Yve. Good to see you." He wipes his bloody hands on a towel looped through the tie of his apron. "You need to use the portal or are you here for some of my world famous pulled pork?"

Mmm, Gold's pulled pork could tempt a Rabbi to sin. They also make a mean shrimp salad, to totally thumb their noses at being kosher.

"I have an appointment with the Man, millennia in the making."

Sol's porcupine brows raise and his jaw slips, jowls jiggling when it bottoms out. "You mean…"

"Yep, I delivered number one million ten minutes ago. Time to cash in." I give him a half-smile. The smoky aroma of slow-roasted pork and tangy barbeque sauce tantalizes my nostrils. My mouth waters like a rabid Pavlov's dog.

Poor Sol. He's been at this game for less than half a century and already he looks so weary and consumed. The Man drives a hard, and often one-sided, bargain. Once upon a time, I thought a million souls easily doable. I should have done the math. Even if I'd delivered a soul a day, a million days is nearly three thousand years. After a while, a girl gets tired of having sex with a series of strangers. When I first started, three a day was a slow pace. Even three at a time wasn't unusual during the Roman orgies. Now, I'm lucky if I can muster the energy to snag three a week. A barbeque sandwich is more likely to paint an orgasmic grin on my face than a decent fuck is.

Sol motions for me to step behind the counter and lead the way to the meat locker. He'll let me out the portal door and reseal it from his side. Returning is much more complex.

As he passes to undo locker's latch, he does a quick perusal of my attire. "Is that what you're wearing?"

I pause and survey my Seven for All Mankind jeans, Manolo Blahnik boots and Missoni knit top. "What? You don't think he'll approve?"

Sol sighs and shakes his head. "You've known him longer than I, of course. I'm sure Lou will be fine with dungarees, a schleppy top and go-go boots."

I run a hand over my ass, round and tight, my second best asset, next to my cootchie and followed closely by my tits. "These make my butt look fantastic, and Missoni is never schleppy."

He pats me on the arm. "Then you have nothing to worry about, Yve."

Inside the meat locker, we weave amongst the pigs dangling from the ceiling, large lumps of porcine carnage. We stop in a far corner of the locker, an unassuming, perfectly camouflaged area. I'd have never guessed it to be a portal to Hell.

"Is anyone meeting you on the other side?"

"Someone's always stationed at the portal. I'm more concerned with who it'll be." I adjust my sweater and straighten my hair. "Last time I went, I had the Hellhound as my guide. Even with three heads, he's not much of a talker and has absolutely *no* sense of humor."

Sol grips each of my shoulders. "Go safely, my dear." He busses both cheeks before taking them in his hands. "A Gold's special on the house will be waiting for you when you return."

Dear Sol. I do hope I return to enjoy that sandwich. I suck in a confidence-shoring breath and step through.

People think Hell is hot, but it's actually cold, cut through you and ice your joints into frozen submission cold. I shiver and hug myself. The entrance appears to be unguarded, but I know that's a false illusion. Lou never leaves his lair open to any schmuck or avenging angel who might stumble or sneak in.

I jog to speed up my visit and to pump some warmth into my body.

"Yve. Long time no sssssseeeee."

I stop. I recognize the voice. "Show yourself, Ta'avah!" This time I will not fail, will not be beguiled by his antics. I have too much at stake.

"Sssweet, sweet Yve. I've missssssed you."

"Ta'avah! Take me to Lou. I command you! Besides, it's only been a week since you last saw me, so cut the theatrics."

He can't disobey an order to take me to his master. Despite the chaos that forms the fabric of Lou's dominion, a few rules are inviolable. Rule number one is all visitors must be brought to Lou, dead or alive. Since I prefer to be alive, I am prepared for a challenge.

"Ssssweet, sssexy, Yve." Ta'avah emerges from the shadows, his breath a fog in the icy air. Lou's chief succubus-maker always appears to me in the form most likely to waylay and tempt me from my end goal. Sadly for me, he usually succeeds. Today, he's tall and muscular with dark curly hair. His aquamarine eyes are framed by nearly black lashes and brows. An angular jawline sports a light dusting of stubble, just enough to be drop dead sexy. Naked from the waist up, his broad shoulders and solid chest invite my fingers to touch. They itch to stroke the fine dark hairs outlining his pectoral muscles and trailing in a narrow column down his stomach where they fan out below his navel. Navel? I burst into a fit of giggles.

"Ta'avah. You have a belly button." My laughter reaches near hysteria and I hiccup trying to make myself stop.

He grins and peers down at the mockery of a birth that never happened. "Don't you like it?" He flexes a bicep and tightens his abdominal muscles into a six pack. The effect snatches a gasp from me. Ta'avah gives a soft chuckle and dips his thumbs in his pockets, fingers pointing to his crotch, a rather sizeable bulge. "This is for you too."

Damn, how did he know? "I'll bet. But I need to see Lou first."

He strolls toward me, a swagger of virile confidence in every step. Eyes scrape up and down my body. "Come on." He starts to walk down the yellow brick road, Lou's sick little attempt at sarcasm. "Rumor has it you delivered your millionth."

I don't like the way he says this. Caution is warranted. "Yep."

"So you're here for redemption, right?" He stops, and I hesitate beside him.

"That's the plan."

A smile infused with something—longing, sadness—curls the edges of his face. "Good for you." Another laugh fills the air. "Good for you." His voice trails off.

THE SUCCUBUS CHRONICLES

Chapter Two

Soon we come to Lou's palace, decked out in opulent excess. I stop to admire the view. For a snake in the grass, Lou's tastes are refined, though a Taj Mahal replica is a smidge over the top.

Ta'avah sidles up to me and pushes a stray lock of my hair behind my ear, then whispers: "You have one last task, my dear. Boss says he wants a front row seat for your last one."

I pull away and whirl on him. "No! I've delivered my million. I'm done." He shakes his head throughout my protest.

"Check your contract." From his back pocket, he removes a single sheet of paper, folded into fourths, and hands it to me, page seventy-nine of eighty-one. The master of subterfuge at his finest. "I marked the pertinent section for you."

I read. *Shit!* "Upon the deliverance of the millionth soul, undersigned agrees to undergo a reversal ceremony under the supervision of Granting Contractor." A girl forgets these types of details after nearly four millennia. *Why me?*

"You don't have to look so fucking happy, Ta." I shift from foot to foot and try to convince myself it could have been much worse. I might have had to fight one or more demons to the death just to reach Lou's palace. I have before. "Where is Lou anyway?"

"I'm here, Lilith's child." Lou emerges from a darkened room to the right, the hissing of undead heralding his exit from their midst. "You have served me well, succubus. Are you ready for your redemption ceremony?"

"I am. Let's get on with it, please."

Lou hikes one corner of his mouth and points to a room on my left. "This way. Ta'avah has a special treat for you."

"I'll bet he does," I mutter under my breath. I shoot a glance at Ta, but his face is inscrutable. There are worse men, or creatures, to fuck while Lou watches. At least I think, I hope, it'll be Ta. He was my initiation demon, after all.

"He can hear you, you know," Ta says in a muted tone.

Ta leads us into a crimson-walled room. In the center is huge pit littered with pillows. Around the sides of the pit are at least ten lounge chairs. The chamber soars two stories, and at the top, windows allow viewers to peer down.

I spin to face Lou. "The contract says under your supervision, not all your minions'."

Lou laughs. "We are legion." His teeth are perfect pearls of brilliance that contrast with his bronzed skin. Sandy blonde hair with platinum highlights surrounds a beautiful face that belies the evil inside. Lou capitalizes on his silky tongue and gorgeous good looks to entrance his victims. Once upon a time I fell and fell hard for his melodious persuasions. Biggest mistake I ever made.

I hold up a hand. "Alright. Let's get it over with."

"Now, there's the spirit," he purrs. He drops down into the pit where he makes himself comfortable on a collection of cushions against the side.

Ta advances on me, a lecherous smile on his face, eyes that bore into mine. "Take off your clothes, Yve."

"Go sit down, over there, first." I point to the opposite side from where Lou lies stretched out.

Ta shakes his head, but does as I ask, his long strides eating up the distance.

"You always were coy," Lou says then yawns.

I lean over in profile to both Lou and Ta and remove my boots, then my jeans and sweater. I fold the garments and place them beneath my footwear. I paid a gazillion dollars for those boots and want to be able to grab them and run if necessary. The rest doesn't matter as much.

Ta sits on the edge of the pit and removes his shoes, Mephistos, of course. What a suck up.

I stroll over in my bra and underwear, Jockey French cut, the modern woman's granny panties. The expression on Ta's face is priceless. "Shut up! I didn't think I'd be entertaining."

"Nice, Yve. Now take 'em off," he demands.

On the one hand, I want to torment Ta, but on the other, I want to get his rocks off and get the hell out of Hades. The sane side wins, and I strip off the undies and toss them near my pile of clothes.

From the corner of my eye, I see Lou perk up and adjust his position. Overhead, faces appear one by one at the viewing glass. The show has begun.

"Come here." Ta unfastens the top button of his pants, then points to the rest. "I got it started for you." What a peach.

I drop to my knees in front of him. We make eye contact. I try to erase my face of any emotion. Ta sports a know-it-all smirk. I don't even want to know what Lou looks like. I unzip Ta's pants with a slow and steady snick, snick, snick. He exhales softly and threads his fingers through my hair.

"All for you, my sweet, sweet succubus. Let's make you last time your best." Ta keeps his voice low and intimate.

Off come his jeans. He's not wearing any underwear. A half-formed erection greets me. I lift my eyes to his and scowl. He shrugs. Son of a bitch is going to make me work for this. *Fine.*

I grasp his cock and give it a few vigorous pumps with my hand. That gets Ta's blood flowing enough to give me something decent to work with. Some artists work with oils and canvas; I work with dicks. I bring my lips to the head of his penis and use my tongue to sweep up and around.

Ta moans, right on cue.

I lick his frenulum, feather-like flicks against the narrow ridge of skin, all the while moving my hand firmly along his shaft.

He moans louder.

I work up some saliva to lubricate my canvas.

Ta sucks in his breath with a staccato-like rhythm. Someone's had a dry spell, methinks.

My mouth slides lower, my tongue like a car wash brush in hyper drive.

Ta's hands curl and relax in a lazy rhythm as I bob up and down on his cock, my fist around the base of his shaft. I slip an occasional finger down to tease his balls. He responds exactly as I hoped.

Normally, I'd be wired by now, ready for my own turn at the fun, but with an audience, it's hard to work up the enthusiasm. I concentrate instead on giving the best blowjob of my life. Ta seems to agree with my efforts because his hips are pumping his cock into my mouth with increasing speed.

From the corner of my eye, I spy a ring of demons forming around the perimeter of the pit. A couple of them openly masturbate as their eyes lap up the scene. They make animalistic growls and grunts.

The loud clapping of hands interrupts me. "Enough!" Lou yells for us to stop, so I stop. Ta looks like he's about to cry. "Watching BJs bores me. Fuck her now, Ta'avah. And make it good."

I drop to my hands and knees, hoping Ta follows my lead. In this position, I can duck my head low and avoid making eye contact with everyone, especially Ta.

He slides his hands over my ass, stroking my skin from the small of my back to the tops of my thighs. I lower my head to present higher to him. "Come on, Ta." My body responds and sends a wave of warmth to prime my snatch for an invasion of the male kind.

Ta maneuvers into position behind me, his cock nudging against my cleft. I rock backward to move him inside.

More demons join in and jack off, hissing with enthusiasm. I'm not liking this type of applause. Gang bangs with boorish demons aren't my thing.

"Oh, Yve, damn baby, you're as hot as an oven." Ta shoves forward and fills me. His hands encircle my waist to hold me steady to receive him again and again. "Oh yeah, you like that don't you, baby?"

I give him a sour look over my shoulder. I hope we don't have to do the hokey sex-a-logue for Lou and his kids.

Ta's eyes close and his head rolls back. I brace myself as he picks up speed and jackhammers me. I close mine too, to shut out the world and welcome the cascading sensations Ta evokes. It works because, like a roller coaster, the tension begins its slow climb to a peak that promises a mind-blowing plummet.

"Change positions!" Lou's bare feet are at my eye level. His toenails are so gnarly even the ladies of Little Saigon Nail Emporium would run screaming.

Ta pulls out with a squishy pop and throws me to my back on a sea of pillows. Out of habit, my legs splay to receive him. He doesn't disappoint and in seconds, he's back inside, thrusting furiously, matching each movement with a primal grunt. I clutch the pillows and again concentrate on the mounting waves of bliss. Despite the circumstances, Ta's using all the right moves. I sense his nearing climax and start to tighten up, priming for my release.

"Not fucking missionary style!" Lou's back and he kicks Ta off of me and onto his back. "Ride this piece of shit, Yve."

I oblige because woman on top is my favorite position. I can make a man come lickety-split when I'm in the saddle. I'm wicked good at driving them a little insane in the membrane once I get to rockin'.

From my new position, I see seven demons surround the pit. Four are having sex with each other, one hetero and one homo pair. One has already shot his wad and left a big mess at his feet. Its hand strokes its shaft in long silky finishing movements. After a final drawn out groan, the demon takes a lounge chair.

Above us, at least a dozen faces peer through the glass. That's all I can see of them, thank goodness.

I impale myself on Ta's cock, swelled to immense proportions. My arousal allows me to take all of him inside without any discomfort. Despite being part of a sex show, he feels wonderful. As I rise and fall on his turgid rod, a warm friction grows and tugs at the hood of my clit. Nerve endings send happy signals to my brain as ripples of bliss come in increasingly shorter, more intense intervals.

"Yeah, Yve, just like that, girl." Ta bucks his hips beneath mine, trying to squeeze inside me a few more centimeters.

I ride him, a lazy trail ride at first, gentle undulations in the saddle. His eyelids flicker, hands grip my hips to squeeze the most from each stride.

I want to keep my verbal expressions of pleasure locked in silence in my head, but they burst out. "Oh-oh-oh," I yell in rhythm with my quickening movements. Ta always amazes me with what a fantastic fuck he is. "Oh yes!" I'm being dragged to pleasure Armageddon. I haven't the strength to stop the orgasm that peeks around the corner, not that I'd want to. Pressure builds. My muscles coil tighter in preparation for the explosion that will free them.

Lou moves in front of me. He's nude and so handsome I momentarily lose track of where I am, even momentarily forget that Ta's beneath me. Lou takes a step to the side and holds his cock in front of my face, engorged and demanding attention. "Suck me," Lou says. It's not a request but somehow I don't care.

THE SUCCUBUS CHRONICLES

Chapter Three

My lips part and I lean toward Lou, close enough to kiss the massive head of his cock, close enough to slide my lips down further.

"More!" he says, pushing his hips forward.

Around us the room erupts into a chorus of "More, more."

I relax my lips and his cock surges forward, ramming against the back of my throat. I nearly gag, but manage to check myself. Lou does not allow gagging. Lou does not allow that which distracts from his own pleasure.

The crowd voices its approval, and before I can shut it out and give Lou what he wants, I catch snippets of, "Fuck her mouth, Lou!" and "Teach that succubus who's boss!"

Lou doesn't acknowledge any of them, just barks deep commands to go faster, slower, harder, deeper. He holds me by the hair and yanks on it like the reins to a horse, guiding my movements how he wants. He's thick and long, but he glides in and out of my mouth with the grace of a dancer until he hits the back of my throat.

"Head back!" Lou orders with a snarl.

I comply and his cock rams deeper inside me, down my throat, invading and taking possession of as much of me as it can, Lou's way of proclaiming he still owns and controls my body. True, but he doesn't own my head or my heart, and as of today, he no longer owns my soul.

Ta stills beneath me, as if he knows I can only deal with so much at once, knows I can neither utter a word nor whimper to protest Lou's final conquest, not with my freedom on the line. Ta is the only one I'll miss from this hellhole, the only one.

Lou laughs before finally backing off some, releasing my hair and lowering my head to a more comfortable angle. His thrusting slows to a sensuous pace.

Beneath me, Ta begins to move again. The thrill of having one dick in my pussy and one in my mouth invigorates me. This is the solitary wisp of power I hold, the ability to own their pleasure, if only for these precious few seconds. Both men vocalize their ecstasy. I close my eyes and beckon my own to come and sit a spell. The three of us move in tandem. One thrusts into me pushing me toward the other who volleys me back. They could be fucking each other through me. My mouth waters. My sex floods. We ripple one to the other, and a hush falls over the room.

All is bliss, until Lou pulls abruptly out of my mouth. "Lie forward." His words come out raspy and strained.

I open my eyes to see him holding his cock in his hand, angry and red and glistening from having been in my mouth. A long string of my saliva still connects us. I comply with his command while Ta continues to thrust into me from beneath.

Lou walks behind me and caresses my bottom, spreads something wet and gooey all around my anus. I'm not sure I want to know what he used, but I'm pretty sure I know what's coming next.

A finger slips inside my sensitive outer ring, then past the second inner ring. A second and third finger plunges deep within me and they fan out inside, opening me wider with each flexing. I cry out at the intimate invasion, anxious of what will come next when the fingers are removed.

"I'm going to fuck you up the ass now, Yve. I'm going to fuck you hard while Ta keeps plowing your beautiful pussy. You can take two cocks at once. Hell, you can probably take three or more, can't you?"

Lou doesn't wait for an answer because I don't have a say in the matter. He's always told me this day would come, that his final sendoff always involved one good long screwing of his former slave. With a loud grunt, he penetrates my rectum with his cock. He feels much larger than he did in my mouth.

Ta ceases his movements, and once Lou has worked his full hard length inside me, he too stills. I'm filled to bursting from the double penetration. The sensation burns at first, but I refuse to scream. Soon the pain abates and thrilling memories of prior threesomes rush in. Around us, the demons break the silence and hiss their approval of the ménage before them.

"Fuck her, Lou," one yells.

"You like that, succubus?" another one calls out.

Lou pulls back and drives forward even deeper. The hairs on his groin brush my lower back. He leans forward, closer to my ear and growls, "I'm going to fuck you like the filthy little cunt you are, and you're going to love every fuckin' second of it." Hips grind against my ass at the bottom of each successive stroke.

Ta also begins to move. "So tight. Won't last much longer." His eyes are squeezed shut and his breath comes in rapid pants.

Both men groan as they enter into a synchronized rhythm of taking turns thrusting inside me, slow and deep. The huffs and moans of every aroused creature in the room, independent but harmonized, blend with my own.

I want to hate what they're doing to me, want to hate those who ogle, but I can't. I'm off the carnal charts.

My brains curdle into mush. My eyelids droop, mouth falls open, and my face contorts with the rushing pressure. Rising mushroom clouds of joy overtake and consume me.

Lou pauses and Ta accelerates his thrusts. I'm going into meltdown when Ta finally loses it. His seed shoots into me in rapid pulses. Lou resumes where Ta leaves off.

"Saved-the-best-for-last!" His grunted words punctuate each thrust, give me that final push into orgasmic oblivion. Lou unleashes a hoarse cry then halts. He holds me tight to take the full force of his ejaculation, hot and copious. Two cocks pulse inside me, and it's too much, too much. The edges of my consciousness wink then fade before I spiral into utter nothingness.

When I come to, Lou's gone. It's just me and Ta and … a dozen demons that don't look too friendly. The ones who enjoyed the show are writhing in the final throes of their own erotic adventures. They pose no threat. The bastardized hybrids of beast and man, however, scare the bejeezus out of me.

"Get dressed while I hold them off," Ta mutters, barely moving his lips. He buttons and zips up, staring down the bolder demons that move a mite too close. The monster-type aren't clever but they're persistent and deadly when the spirit moves. Their kind also tends to follow a pack mentality—when one attacks, they all attack.

I tug my own clothes on with supersonic speed, ditching the underwear. Before I slip on my boots, I remove the two church-blessed daggers I have concealed in the shank of each boot. I never visit Hell unarmed.

When I spin around, Ta holds an ax in one hand and a knife in the other. He's also slipped on a shirt he either hid or stole. He takes in my status and nods. "You retain the title of smartest succubus I ever created."

"High praise, indeed," I say.

"If we can make it to the door of the palace, I can seal it from the outside. That'll give us a small head start, hopefully enough to get us to the portal."

"Why are you helping me instead of them?" I wave my dagger at a lecherous satyr who takes a swipe at me but only snags my hair.

"Because, my sweet Yve, you are not the only one who has fulfilled a contract." Ta delivers a roundhouse kick to a second satyr who tries to sneak up on him. With a loud screech, it falls to the floor and is set upon by two dragon-like demons that rip it in half.

"What? You're a conscript? You were human once?" All this time, I'd thought Ta a minion. I'd no idea, he'd bargained his way into the job of chief succubus-maker.

"A conscript bound to deliver a billion souls for my freedom through the succubi I made. Your millionth was my billionth plus one for extra security. I chose you well, Yve. You were my first, my favorite." His smile is boyish with a hint of pride. The heart I thought frozen solid thousands of years ago thaws enough to release a slow drip of water.

THE SUCCUBUS CHRONICLES

Chapter Four

"Let's get the hell out of here then," I say to Ta.
"On my signal... Now!"

I bolt for the door. Two drooling, fanged demons covered in thick pelts of black dreadlocks try to block my path. A stab in the gut transforms them into shrieking balls of fur and teeth. Four demons pounce and finish them off. The rest pursue. Ta spins to take out one of the speed demons.

"Keep going, I'll be right behind you!" he yells.

I do, taking out three foul-smelling trolls who charge as I enter the front lobby. My flight skids to halt, however, when the front door refuses to open.

"Go!" Ta shouts as he finishes off a large attacker with the head of a komodo dragon and the body of an orangutan. I hear its death howls and Ta's approaching footfall.

"It won't open!" I shriek tugging on the door handle.

"It's warded. Say 'Owa'a Teygu'u Siyam' three times while spinning and it'll open."

"What? Okay." I do as Ta says and when I finish, he's standing next to me flipping a series of latches I'd not noticed. The door swings free.

He chuckles and motions me through, slamming the door behind us. From his pocket, he produces a padlock he uses to secure an external latch. "Owa'a Teygu'u Siyam!" He claps his hands three times then clicks the lock shut. When he says the words, they sound suspiciously like 'Oh what a goose I am.' Damn him. I'm such an idiot.

"There was no magic ward on the door, was there?" I cross my arms in front of my chest, the points of my two daggers pointed to the sky.

"Nope. But you sure were cute spinning around, confessing your mental slowness." A peal of laughter erupts and has to run its course before he takes my hand and says, "Come on, Miss Fois Gras. Let's get out of here before Lou sics any more nasties on us."

"I can't believe we've finally ended our contracts with the Man himself." I blink a few times as I shake my head.

The incredulity on Ta's face removes my smile. "Wait. All this time you thought Lou was Lucifer, Beelzebub, Mephistopheles, the Big Kahuna?"

"Isn't he?"

Ta throws his arm around my shoulder. "Oh honey. Lou is a lesser demon at best, middle management. Seven portals, seven districts, seven Lous. They report to the greater, regional demons. Above them is the Demonic Council. The Council reports to the Head of the Damned. The Damned is the largest department, of course, but others include the Departments of Pestilence, Natural Disasters, the Apocalypse, the Fallen, who refuse to be lumped together with the Damned—"

"Fuck me…"

"Any time."

We make our way to the portal unmolested but find it barred by an army of foot-long scorpions.

"What now?" I crouch behind a boulder with Ta and watch them patrol, their eight legs clicking a tattoo on the golden bricks.

Ta hesitates, studying the scorpions. I know that look, a trickster's mind spinning the fine filaments of a plot to deceive. "Mating season approaches. Perhaps I can accelerate the calendar. Once they start, they'll be too busy dancing and mating to pay us much attention. The females will devour the males, further culling the ranks until the next generation comes."

"How are you going to do that?"

"I am the master of pheromones of all species, my dear. Humans aren't the only ones I can turn into succubi."

"Ewww."

"Hopefully I have enough powder left. Take notes from the master and learn."

Ta closes his eyes and hums. A curious scorpion crawls over to investigate, and when it's almost upon us, Ta blows a greenish cloud of powder on it. "Let's hope it's a she."

The scorpion stops, turns in a circle and arches its stinger in a complete loop. Pincers elevated, it clicks back to its brethren. Two other scorpions immediately surround it.

"Bingo," Ta whispers. "The other females will follow suit, not wanting to be the last to seek a mate and finding only the dregs."

"I never stood a chance against you, did I?"

"Not a whit." The crooked curl of his smile triggers a fluttery jig in my gut. "But I never stood a chance against you either." His smile fades. "I *am* sorry, Yve."

I roll my eyes and nudge him in the arm. "All water under the bridge now, isn't it. But thank you, Ta. You've actually been an okay master."

He releases a soft snort and gazes at me sidelong. "Just okay?" A little boy dances behind the warm eyes resting on me.

I bob my head from side to side. "If they made a greeting card to say thank you and goodbye to your succubus maker, I'd have purchased it for you, Ta, but I doubt they get much call for that sort of thing."

"Probably not, though Delia baked me a cake after her redemption."

My head snaps his way. "What? Wait. How many of your succubi have been redeemed?" All this time I'd assumed I was his first redemption since I was his first succubus.

"Counting you?" His eyes roll up and his lips move as he works through some sort of computation. "Carry the five, makes ... six hundred and sixty six."

"Ha ha. Very funny. Seriously though."

He faces me, his expression totally sober. "Yve. You were my first succubus, but you're my last redemption."

"What?" I can't wrap my head around what he's telling me. I reflect on my track record of soul harvests. Sure I had a few slumps but for millennia I was a busy, busy succubus, one of the busiest. No way could *all* of his subsequent succubi have worked faster than me. "How is this possible? Are you telling me I've been riding the short bus for succubi all this time?"

He shifts and licks his lips. A hand rises to smooth back his hair. He can't or won't meet my eyes.

"Ta? Talk to me."

"Well, every contract is different. A couple were renegotiated. There may have been a few sweepstakes—"

I press two fingers to his lips. "How many souls did the six hundred and sixty *fifth* succubus harvest?"

"Uh, she was a special case, you know, not really indicative of the typical contract—"

"How many?" I check my volume when a scorpion hisses a few feet away from us. "How many?" I repeat in a softer voice.

"A thousand."

"Son of a bitch! A measly thousand? Seriously?" My lower jaw is too heavy to move into the closed position. It hangs in space, numb and lifeless.

Ta shoots me a pained look. "Like I said, she was a special case, not typical."

"Okay then, how many other succubi had a million soul quota like me?"

This time he doesn't even hesitate. "You were the only one."

"And the next highest was?" I lower my chin and fix him in my laser sights.

He shrugs. "Maybe a half million … ish."

"Geesh, Ta. I can't believe this." I want to throttle him, but now isn't the time. There will be plenty of time for that later, once we get out of here, if we get out of here. "And how long have you been waiting for my millionth soul?"

He squints and purses his lips. "I think Debbie had her redemption ceremony in nineteen seventy eight."

"Over thirty years ago. Wow. Just…wow." Ta *had* been underfoot more these past few years. "How come you said you had to check on your girls, plural the last few times you visited me?"

"Julie's a wolf, the alpha female of her pack. She lives in the woods just north of where you live. She was just practice material. That's all. The succubus critters don't have soul contracts, obviously." He offers nothing further. I don't think I want to hear any more anyway.

"The scuttling noises have nearly stopped." I rise up to take a look. Ta pops up next to me.

We spy as the mating frenzy slowly diffuses throughout the ranks. Most of the scorpions have paired off and danced into more secluded areas. The path to the portal is clear.

Ta touches my arm and gazes into my eyes. "You do know, once you step through to the other side, you'll be fully human again, right? Your ability to stave off aging and to regenerate from injury and disease will be gone."

I nod. I am so ready to grow old and finally rest, ready to earn my redemption from the mortal world, one day at a time. Though there's still enough devil in me to want to hurt Ta for this massive fraud he's perpetrated on me. All these years I have labored under the delusion that all succubi were alike, only to discover that for some, their time had been nothing more than a sexy vacation.

I take Ta's hand and we dash toward the portal. A couple of crusty old bachelors challenge us, but Ta's and my swift kicks eliminate the pitiful threats. We're nearly ready to jump through the portal when a hand locks on my arm and jerks me back.

"Ta!" I scream and struggle against the hand I now see is attached to one of Lou's right hand men. "Let me go, Raziel! I've paid my dues! I've been redeemed!"

Raziel stands nearly seven feet tall—as mean as he is huge. He snarls and drags me closer, close enough to give me a noxious whiff of his breath. *Ugh*. Carrion mixed with cigarettes, coffee and rotten teeth.

Ta is nowhere to be seen. The bastard must have jumped through the portal and left me behind. Why am I surprised? He's always stuck it to me in some form or fashion. And yet, I am surprised. His betrayal saps all the fight from me.

"We found an accounting error. You owe Lou one more soul." Raziel grins, the rotten relics of his teeth like rows of tree stumps smeared in shit.

"I do not! My records are meticulous. And dude! Doesn't Lou have a dental plan for you guys?"

Raziel actually looks hurt. "Shut the fuck up." He gives me a rude shove and I am stumbling back to Lou's for a second time.

THE SUCCUBUS CHRONICLES

Chapter Five

Lou sits behind his desk looking immaculate as usual. He's reading something and doesn't even look up when Raziel drags me inside and dumps me in a chair. Raziel takes his post immediately behind me.

Lou raises the papers and taps them into order before leveling his dark eyes upon me. "Yve. Back for more, I see." A grin spreads across his face, claiming as much of the real estate as possible. The smile fades, and he cocks his head to the side. "You short-changed me, tried to cheat me."

"I did not! I kept meticulous records, Lou!"

He slams a fist on his desk and stands. "Not meticulous enough. I don't like to be cheated. Nobody cheats me!" Less than a second later he's standing in front of me, my chin in his hand. "Especially not by a temptress who had nothing more complicated to do than spread her legs."

My jaw tenses. I'm sick of the attitude that succubi are no more than walking vaginas with a top notch advertising campaign. I've put up with the snickers and sneers from Lou and his demons for four millennia. Even if I owe him one more soul, and I'm sure I don't, I refuse to let him devalue me like this. "Show me your records to compare to mine. I think *you're* trying to cheat *me*."

Behind me Raziel sucks in an audible breath through his teeth. I'm sure he thinks my challenging Lou is unwise. He's probably right, but I can't help myself.

Lou releases my chin and walks back behind his desk. "The fellow in Macy's? Earlier today in the men's dressing room? Remember him?"

I do. He had the tiniest prick I'd ever seen, but somehow he managed to get off. "Yeah. Joe, he said his name was."

"That's the one." Lou snaps his fingers, retakes his seat and chuckles. "You're losing your touch, Yve, because ol' Joe faked it."

A frisson of panic takes control. "What do you mean?"

"Faked it, as in he didn't have an orgasm." Lou places both palms against his cheeks. "No O? Oh no!" He snickers. Raziel joins him in his mockery of me.

"No way!"

"You know the rules, Yve," Lou says shaking his head sadly.

"But you got his soul. I delivered that to you." My panic has risen to just below my nose, nearly high enough to drown me.

Lou steeples his fingers and leans forward. "No. Your bargain with your prey is their soul for an orgasm while having sex with you. No orgasm for them, no soul for me, which leaves you one short, an oversight you nearly got away with until my eagle-eyed accountant told me he'd had a last minute soul reversion due to noncompliance. Lo and behold, it was one of yours."

I clench my eyes shut and press my lips together. "Okay. Fine. I'll leave, get one more and we'll finally be done." I rise to stand but two strong hands push me back down.

"I don't think so. A thousand more souls or your ass goes into my harem for the next year. Your choice. Either option is quite generous on my part, I must say." Lou pushes a contract across the desk to me, the same papers he had been perusing when I first entered his office.

Shit! I can't believe this is happening. I'd cry but I lost that ability when Ta converted me. That I even remember crying is distressing all by itself.

I do the math. A thousand souls if collected one a day will take nearly three years. Three more years of sex with a slew of faceless, nameless men or one year with Lou. Sex with Lou, however, is never vanilla, but a terrifying and kinky imbalance of pleasure and pain, joy and despair, enlightenment and horror…and he is not stingy about sharing his toys with his favorite minions.

The contract contains the usual mumbo jumbo but is at least twice as long as the contract Ta'avah tricked me into signing. A good lawyer would need a week to dissect it. I don't have a week, but I also know if sign, loopholes could keep me imprisoned far beyond the thousandth soul. But what choice do I have?

My shoulders slump and I sigh. "Can I borrow your pen?"

"Don't sign that!" a voice cries out.

I turn to the source of the warning. Ta is striding toward me. Raziel spins to block him but Ta blows some sort of powder in his face then points out the door he's left open behind him. "Raziel! Look! A virgin! Out in the hallway!"

Raziel grunts and charges out of the room, tackling a she-demon with blue skin and red eyes to the ground. Ta slams the door but not before I hear the demon's cackles and Raziel's lusty roars.

"Let her go, Lou. She's fulfilled her contract," Ta says. He's breathless like he's been running.

"Ta'avah. Why in Satan's name would you dare show your face back here?"

"Yve has delivered a million souls as of today." Ta moves stand at the edge of the desk.

"Mmm, I'm afraid not. She had a misfire with her last one in Macy's this morning. That means she's shy one soul. But no worries, I've given her a new agreement to sign and all this ugliness will be behind us."

"I'm not talking about that needle-dicked jerk you sent. Oh yes, I know all about 'Joe' and your little plot. I thought something was odd about that guy from the word go. Now, of course, it all makes sense. You were the one who tried to cheat, not Yve. But, no matter. That schmuck wasn't her millionth." He places his two fists on Lou's desk and leans forward, barely a foot separating their faces. "I was."

I'm totally confused. What is Ta talking about? We had sex as part of my redemption ceremony, but I hardly think that counts. A quick glance at Lou, though, tells me there's a lot more to this that I understand. I'm all ears.

Lou sits back down and smirks at Ta. "You'll hand over your newly won soul, return to your former fallen state for this," he points at me, "pathetic creature?"

What the hell is Lou talking about? My eyes dart back and forth between Ta and Lou, but my brain can find no sense in their words.

"Yes, but I propose a trade. My wings for my soul," Ta says, a ferocious note in his voice.

"Without your wings, you'll grow old and die like the rest of them, and for what? I'll probably still get your soul on Judgment day."

"I know, but that makes it an offer you can't refuse, doesn't it?"

"You'd do that? For *her*?" Lou's brow is furrowed, the usual mischievous glint in his eyes gone, replaced by something cold and evil. "Why?"

Ta curls up half of his mouth in that wry smile that always undoes me. "You wouldn't understand.

You're incapable of understanding, Lou." He reaches a hand behind him toward me. "Come on, Yve. We're leaving ... for the last time."

"You'll regret this. You will. You'll be back, mark my words, only your deal when you do—when you're old and grey, nearly deaf and blind and aching with every step you take—won't be nearly so sweet as your last one. Think long and hard before you make such a foolish sacrifice."

Ta pulls me from the chair and tucks me under one of his arms. "I won't be back. And if I were you, I'd start rounding up all the favors I was owed because you're going to need them."

We back away toward the door. Lou pushes back from his chair. "What are you talking about?" he asks.

Do I hear a hint of nervousness? From Lou?

Ta smirks but we keep moving. "Let's just say a certain Demonic Council will be very interested in a ledger that will be delivered to them if I don't step through the portal to recall it in about," he checks his watch, "fifteen minutes. This ledger doesn't quite match up to the one you've been reporting from. I'm certain the Demonic Council will find its contents ... fascinating."

Lou pales and takes on a greenish tinge. His eyes narrow to near slits. Lips roll back to reveal a row of needle sharp teeth, while his surfer blonde hair thins to a few wispy strands in the worst comb-over imaginable. The last glimmer of the façade he usually wears vanishes, and the demon standing in front of us wearing Lou's tailor-made suit, is hideous and foul and very pissed off. Time to go.

Outside of Lou's office I release a shaky breath and show Ta my still quivery hands. He smiles but keeps us moving.

We pass Raziel, who is being spanked and fisted by the blue-skinned she-demon. "Thank you, ma'am, may I have another," he whimpers.

Not only do we meet with no opposition this time, the path is completely clear of hazards, animate or inanimate.

"Are you going to explain what just happened back there, Ta?" I ask as we near the portal.

He sighs. "I wasn't a human conscript but a fallen angel before I became Chief Succubus Maker. Don't ask me about the circumstances that led to my contract with Lou. They are complex and best forgotten. But anyway, Lou took my soul and my wings as collateral until I fulfilled my contract. I got my soul back as soon as you delivered my billionth soul and your next to last one. The wings I could only reclaim after you concluded your contract."

"So explain what happens now that you have a soul but no wings, as a former fallen angel."

"Without them and with the relinquishment of my succubus-making powers, I will become as mortal as you once I leave this place.

"Is that what you want? I mean, if you stay, you could possibly negotiate, as only you can, a way to get them back."

He takes me into his arms and kisses the top of my head. "From the moment I first saw you in that garden so many, many years ago, pissed off as usual at that dolt of an ex-husband of yours, you're all I've ever wanted, all I've ever dreamed about, all I've ever hoped or lived for."

I lean back to gaze into eyes that twinkle not with cunning, but with tenderness, fragile and uncertain. On my tiptoes, I reach up and pull his head to mine and kiss him. He sighs and tightens his hold, deepening the kiss.

Warmth floods every fiber of my being. My soul sings for joy and calls to his, both free at last.

When we finally end the kiss, Ta presses his forehead to mine and cups my cheek. "Are you ready?"

I nod. Holding hands, we jump through the shimmery window separating Hell from Sol's meat locker.

Ta breathes in deeply. "Mmm. What's that smell?"

"That, dear Ta, is heaven in a bun."

"I could say the same about you, my treasure." He winks, his handsome face having retained its last permutation. The strange fluttering in my belly makes an encore, warming my heart. He leans down and kisses me again, and I realize, with soul-shattering intensity that I can no more live without Ta than I can without air to breath or water to drink. As I gaze at him, I also realize that in my thousands of years, Ta has always been there, as much an inseparable part of me as my beating heart.

I link my arm with his and tug him through the door of the meat locker, through the kitchen and into the restaurant. "Come on. Let's go eat. Afterward, I'll take you to my home. You can stay with me… 'til you get on your feet. But first we need to change your name. Ta'avah just doesn't work in this world."

"What would you suggest?"

I tap my finger against my chin in mock contemplation. "I think … Cletus would be perfect, the name of an Adonis. It suits you, Ta."

I pat him on the back and lead him to a secluded table for two in the corner. Our waitress sashays over, but I wave off the menus. "A Gold's special for my oldest, most dearest friend in the whole wide the world and beyond."

THE SUCCUBUS CHRONICLES

DEDICATION

To my sista from another mista, Sandi—thanks for all the moral support. Love ya, girlie.

THE SUCCUBUS CHRONICLES

SUCCUBUS GAMES

Lila Shaw

Copyright © 2012

There are deities who may take you under their wings, making you their protégés of sorts. Form such associations with delicacy and caution for they are rarely for your long-term benefit. Jealousy amongst their kind when unleashed is frequently visited upon the innocent.
"I'm With The Gods," Adventures of an Olympian Groupie by Pamela D'Mar

Chapter One

I learned the hard way to stay out of fights that don't concern me. The memories of those you support are extremely short and those you oppose extremely long. And if they're petulant gods from Mount Olympus, well, you can kiss your ass goodbye.

Sisyphus Prison has been my home for centuries, and neither its landscape nor its inhabitants do much to recommend the place. A few are interesting fellows, who, like me, are only guilty of being caught between two bickering deities.

Every year the gods descend and watch our games, the highlight of which is this gladiator-type match where the winner is granted his or her freedom, and the loser is banished to Tartarus, the underworld of Hades. The wardens hold a lottery to determine the combatants. Competition to play in the Games of Sisyphus is fierce because anywhere, even the underworld, is better than Sisyphus.

Standing in the center square with hundreds of others, I rip open my envelope and stare at my ticket, number 1811. I lift my chin into the gentle breeze and smile to the heavens. 1811 is the date of the Games in reverse, surely a lucky omen. "Thank you, Aphrodite," I whisper to my patroness, the goddess of love, though I doubt she's listening.

Tyche hosts the lottery and chooses one lucky winner each year. She's the goddess of chance and fortune, and therefore deemed neutral and objective. Go figure. She doesn't like me though, not since I seduced one of her boy toys. He was a dud, so no huge loss on her part. But really, what did she expect when she sent him to rough me up over a little past due rent? I was, am, a succubus. Sex is my thing, what keeps me alive, and men are my utensils. Poor things don't stand much of a chance when my hunger rages. This quirk of my nature, of course, always makes *me* the evil temptress.

Approaching briskly through the throng of inmates also hoping for their shots at freedom is Narcissus.

"Hey Willow! You ready for the drawing this year?" He pulls out a mirror and fusses with his hair.

"Sure do, Narce. Lucky number 1811. You?" I wave my ticket between his face and the mirror.

He spins out of reach. "Yo girl, course I do. I'm number seven."

"Seven? As in zero-zero-zero-seven? As in you were somehow one of the first ones to get your number?"

He tilts his head. "I don't know why you act so shocked. I told you I'm tight with the warden." A wink hints at exactly *how* close they might be.

"I suppose it doesn't matter since pure chance determines who gets picked, right?"

Narce cocks a brow. "Sister, that's what they want you to believe, but I happen to know they never put more than the first five hundred numbers in the bowl."

My mouth drops. "What? Why not? Who told you this?"

"Tyche just likes to be a bitch, and I heard it from her sister, Nemesis, the tall one with the thinning hair in the back?" He ruffles his own gorgeous locks for emphasis. Never a bad hair day for Narcissus.

I roll my eyes. Narce can be such a queen sometimes. However, his gossip is usually right. I need a ticket under 500 to even have a chance at being selected.

"I don't suppose you'd trade tickets with me?" I bat my eyelashes, but flirting with Narcissus is like offering a light to the sun. The dude only thinks of himself and is impervious to my wiles. Maybe that's why we get along so well—he is as safe from me as I am from him.

He flops his hands on his hips, pokes out his lips and shakes his head.

"Do you know anyone else with a low ticket number?"

Narce screws up his mouth and scans the crowd, eyes squinting.

"Why don't you get glasses so you can see better? Your eyesight's getting worse." I constantly nag him about this, but he never listens.

"Can't break up the perfect lines of my face with something so obnoxious as...ugh...spectacles." He rises on his tiptoes. "Ah, yes! There's one. Helveticus. He showed me his digits—403."

"Does he know about the cutoff?" I step closer to follow Narce's line of sight. I've never met nor heard of this Helveticus guy.

The man in question puts Narce to shame in the looks department, not that Narce would admit it. Helveticus stands nearly six and a half feet tall. Hair of darkest ebony flows down his back but is trapped in a loosely tied leather strap. The locks of hair in front of his ears are tightly braided into thin ropes. A full beard, not too long, not too short, no visible signs of leftover meals tangled within, adorns his face. The white toga he wears sets off his deeply tanned skin and crystal blue eyes. Someone's been hanging out in the Apollo tanning fields. He's strong too, with big, bulgy muscles in his arms, shoulders, chest and calves. I wonder what he did to merit a spot in this wretched place?

"I doubt he's been clued in. You shouldn't have any problem convincing him." Narce pats my back. "Good luck to you, Willow. Win or lose, if you're chosen, you'll be granted a pass out of here." A broad grin overtakes his face. "Then *I'll* be the best-looking one."

Leave it to Narcissus to prize a higher ranking in the beauty poll over his freedom.

Helveticus stands quietly waiting for the drawing, which is not for another hour. He's not talking or reading or doing anything, with his arms dangling at his sides. His calm would have grabbed my attention even if his low number had not.

I glide toward him, my most alluring pout affixed to my face.

"Hi." I step close enough for the pheromones I produce to work their magic.

His gaze drifts up and down my body, lingering on breasts barely covered by my Rufus Lorrie designer toga. Oh yeah, he's hooked.

"Hello." He tears his eyes away and focuses on some object off in the distance.

I follow his sightline to Narcissus flexing his biceps while a bored-looking nymph holds his mirror for him.

"I'm Willow. My friend Narcissus pointed you out to me." I find opening with a truth, accompanied by a healthy dose of love perfume, usually works much better than playing the coquette.

"The fellow with the mirror?" He extends his hand out in front of his face to pantomime Narce's constant companion.

"Yeah, that's the guy. Anyway, he said you were participating in the drawing."

"Everyone here is participating." One brow lifts, the other one hunkers down. He's suspicious.

"Right." I glance around, alert for observers or eavesdroppers. Now comes the lying. "See, here's the thing. I've got this ticket here." I hold up my 1811 ticket. "Only these numbers are very unlucky for me. I've consulted the Oracle and it agrees. So I was wondering ... if you might ... want to switch?" I thrust my breasts forward to recommend them and by extension, my suggestion.

He narrows his eyes. "You want to switch tickets? Why'd you pick me? Why didn't you switch with your friend, Narcissus?"

I sigh. "I asked, but he said 'no' because he was already holding his lucky numbers." I up the 'oomph' of my love juices and smile. "Plus, you're the most attractive man here. Duh!"

Helveticus crosses his arms at his chest. His pectoral muscles flex in an appealing manner, subduing my irritation. "I wasn't born last century, you know. Nearly everyone here is attractive. Most of us are demi-gods; it goes with the territory."

My head falls forward with the weight of his petulance. Why are some men so difficult? Time to get serious. I step closer and reach out a hand to touch his beefy bicep. "True, but you struck my fancy. I can't explain why, but you did. I asked Narcissus who you were, he told me, and here I am."

The wry set of his mouth is not encouraging.

With a groan, I lean in. "Okay. What'll it take to get you to switch tickets with me with no further questions asked?"

A laugh bubbles from those succulent lips of his, lips begging to be kissed. He leans in. "Whatcha got to offer?"

I smile my most seductive grin. "What you see is what I've got. I'm told I'm the best you'll ever have."

Gentle male fingers curl against the curve of my waist leaving glowing embers in their tracks. In a hushed voice he says, "Funny, I'm told the same thing."

Clearly this man woke up with the solitary mission of tousling my world. I should walk away and find someone else. There are 498 other possible candidates, after all, but with only an hour left, my chances of finding one without rousing suspicion are dwindling fast.

I'm stumped at what to do next when Helveticus huffs. "Fine. Show me what you got."

"Oh! So you'll switch tickets with me?"

"No, I'll sell you my ticket for yours in exchange for four hours in my bed—a half hour now and the rest after the drawing."

Helveticus is dealing in my kind of currency. Advantage mine, but I can't seem too eager. "Two hours," I counter.

"Three and a half."

"Three."

He shakes his head and tucks his ticket inside his toga. "Pleasure chatting with you, Willow. Good luck in the drawing." He's nearly ten paces away from me when I catch him.

"Fine. Three and a half hours in your bed." I raise my finger in warning. "But not a single minute until *after* the drawing."

He eyes me sidelong. "Can I trust you?"

"How do you expect me to answer other than with 'of course you can', which you may or may not believe?"

"Point well made." Out comes his ticket, number 403, just as Narce said, but he holds it against his chest.

I am forced to take a step closer to accept his half of the exchange and to hand him my 1811 ticket.

His eyes make a lazy round-trip of my body, from my sandaled feet to the headband in my hair, before returning to bore into mine."17 Pegasus Lane. Meet you there ten minutes after the drawing. Wear something sexy, and I might go easier on you."

I give him a smirk. He won't know what hit him after I bed him. He won't last thirty minutes let alone seven times that and in the arena he'll be as formidable as a pigeon feather. "17 Pegasus Lane. Got it."

"And Willow?"

"Yes?"

"If you don't show up, I will find you. There's a reason I'm in this place, and it has nothing to do with looking cross-eyed at the wrong goddess when she was PMS'ing."

I tilt my head and say, "I said I'd be there, and I will." With a theatrical spin on my heel and a swing of my hips, I go in search of Narce, confident my ass has a new worshipper.

Chapter Two

Narcissus claps when he sees me waving my new ticket in front of my face.

"Oh, hey girl, you are the woman! How did you do it?"

"Once I set my mind to something, I never give up until I get it. Plus, I finagled three hours and change worth of play time." I nudge Narce with my elbow and wink at him.

He laughs, and we gossip for the remainder of the hour about the others gathering closer to the podium where Tyche will ascend and do her thing. Her co-host as usual is Aphrodite.

Narce puts a finger to his lips and points with his other hand. "Shh, shh, here she comes!"

The crowd stills.

Tyche clears her throat. "I'll be brief. As is our tradition, we shall pick two champions, two warriors to fight for the amusement of the gods, yada, yada. You all know this by now, right?"

Murmurs confirming her assumption arise from the crowd.

"It's mostly the same, only I have a new gadget this year. Many thanks to Prometheus for his lovely invention." She moves to a large spinning chamber flanked by two Adonis-like men.

"What's with the invention," I whisper to Narce. "Did Nemesis mention it?"

He shakes his head, eyes wide, mouth parted slightly, and turns back to the stage.

"We've got over two thousand of you represented in there, so let's give it spin shall we boys?" Tyche motions for the twins, who wear nothing but fig leaves over their twigs and berries for a pleasingly full foliage effect. The men turn a crank and the mesh drum rotates.

Inside the see-through chamber, a lot more than five hundred coins tumble and fall, clanking and tinkling against each other.

I shoot a pissed off glare at Narce.

He shrugs. "What can I say? Technology's a bitch."

Tyche scans the crowd, her attention fixed on a man in front. "On each coin is a number. If I pull the coin bearing your number, you are my champion. My co-host, Aphrodite will pull the second coin for her champion."

The man she addresses her words to is Helveticus. He returns her smile. *Oh no.* Please tell me I've not just bargained with Tyche's consort for an afternoon of stamina-leeching sex.

The bin stops spinning, and the twins unlatch the door. Tyche raises a slender arm and extends it into the sea of golden coins. She digs deeply into its depths, and when a smile settles into place, she withdraws the first winning coin. All murmuring ceases as she turns the coin to read the number engraved on its side.

"The first champion of this year's Games of Sisyphus is..." The pause she inserts is brilliantly played judging from the expectant expressions on the faces of those near me, including Narce. "Number 1811!"

Mingled cries of despair and claps for the victor rise up and swallow us. *That's my number!* I think I'm going to faint. I spin to grin at Narce, but he is mouthing, "I'm so sorry."

I glance at the ticket in my hand and remember. I hold 403, not 1811. "Pan's poop! Damn, damn and triple damn!"

Tyche motions for Helveticus to stand beside her on stage. He draws gasps from the maidens, throaty grunts from the older females and admiring glances from a few flamboyant males. Narce appears unfazed, though he checks his mirror. I guess seeking reassurance he is still the fairest in the land is as much of a compliment as another creature can expect from Narce.

"My champion, Helveticus!" Tyche crows.

"This is so rigged," I whisper to Narce.

"It's always rigged," he whispers back.

Helveticus smiles and surveys the crowd. He is a fine specimen of manhood, and despite my irritation at how cruelly the Fates have treated me, I look forward to our session. When our gazes lock, a lightning bolt of sexual awareness travels the few feet separating us and threatens to ignite me. *Oh baby!* A thunderclap of excitement shudders through me in its wake.

"And now for his opponent," Tyche begins, but she pauses to focus her attention on Helveticus. Her gaze follows his and zeroes in on me, eyes narrowed. "If my co-hostess would kindly join me on stage." She clears her throat, and after glancing at Helveticus, angles to her left where my patroness Aphrodite sits buffing her nails.

I have often appealed to Aphrodite seeking my release, but without success. Despite her displays of contrition, I think she wrote me off within a few years of my landing here. She is the reason I'm here, but grudges grow heavy after a while, and I've since offloaded mine. Aph's not a bad gal; she just tends to follow her heart a bit too much.

"My lovely colleague, Aphrodite, will choose the second competitor as *her* champion." Tyche steps back, clapping and waving Aphrodite on to the stage.

Aph splays her fingers across her chest and shakes her head like she's surprised to be called upon but soon acquiesces. A few steps later, and she's at the drum. She gives each of the fig leaf boys a rather lingering kiss before they set the bin to spinning again.

I don't think anyone in the crowd except the very foolish wish to fight Helveticus, not unless they want to play master and servant with Hades. Helveticus is too large and powerful, with a mean glint in his eye. I'd be frightened, but I do enjoy a spicy alpha male.

Tyche and Aph converse while we wait for the coins to cease their tumbling. Aph's beautiful lashes flutter, and the hairs on my neck rise. Whatever the goddesses are discussing, my instincts tell me I should worry.

The spinning ends. Aph moves forward to execute her conscripted task. She removes all her rings before daintily selecting a coin from the surface of the heap.

"Number four—" She leans over to show the coin to Tyche. "Is this an 'O' or a zero?"

Tyche rolls her eyes and declares it to be a zero. Aph's beauty is unparalleled, but she's not the brightest star in the heavens, yet another reason why I'm here.

"Four, oh, I mean zero, three! Four hundred and three!"

Oh my gods, that's me!

Oh shit, that's me.

How the hell am I going to beat Helveticus? So much for winning my freedom. Hades, here I come. Maybe I can just concede so I won't show up on the underlord's doorstep looking like death. Not the best way to make an entrance as a concubine.

But ... I'll be fucking Helveticus for three and a half hours this afternoon. Perhaps the Fates have begun weaving a new pattern for me. If I can drain enough of his energy, I might have a chance. Normally I only take what I need from my sex partners, but with the stakes being what they are, perhaps I need to be more selfish. I wouldn't be the first succubus to leave a man in a near vegetative state after an afternoon romp.

***

Number 17 Pegasus Lane commands the block like a bloated king amidst a court of beanpole jesters. Who's he been banging? Probably Tyche from the looks of their exchange. I suspect she's a generous but demanding patroness. I live on the more squalid side of Sisyphus. So many of Aphrodite's "kids" live here; there is not much support to go around. At least she's more generous than Zeus. That asshole never gives even his favorites the stingiest of donations. No doubt Hera's influence. The smartest move I ever made was to avoid that one. His brother Hades will be bad enough, but at least he's got a sexy bad boy vibe going for him.

Before my knuckles can strike Helveticus's door, it swings open. We stare at each other, me waiting for him to invite me in, he for ... no idea. Maybe he's afraid of Tyche screwing him over if she finds out he's dallying with me. I wonder if he knows I'm a succubus.

"So you're a succubus, I hear?" he says.

Guess that mystery is shot.

He takes my hand and tugs me forward. His other hand slides into the small of my back, and a finger settles into the cleft of my ass.

Warmth from his palm pools briefly against my skin before winging through my body. Heat shoots to the tips of my fingers and toes before rebounding to ignite the space between my legs. *Nice.*

I glance about the room he's invited me into. The ceiling looms high above us and is adorned with various erotic scenes—orgies, autoeroticism, men with women, women with women, men with men. Beneath my feet is an intricate mosaic tile depicting Zeus raping some poor mortal woman. Disgusting what passes for art these days.

"So, are you?" he asks.

"Am I what?"

The edges of his lips lift slightly. "A succubus?"

"Why does it matter?" I breeze past him, away from Zeus toward a vignette of Athena waging one of her many battles. Girl power. I'd rather look at her.

"It makes a difference in how we spend the next three and a half hours, considering we'll be battling each other right after."

I blow out a puff of contemptuous air. "Worried you can't handle me?"

He bursts out laughing. "Oh, sweetheart. Have you got it all wrong."

"Do I? What makes you think so?" I slip off my outer robe.

Helveticus's eyes darken as they romp over the sheer gauze of my gown. I don't often wear my gossamer frock, mostly because I'm worried my lust-crazed partners will rip it. I typically dial back the pheromones until my designer confection lies safely in a puddle at the foot of a bed.

"You really don't know who I am, do you?" The distance between us shrinks, his sandals barely audible on the tile floor.

I tilt my head to stare at him, and lick my lips seductively. "No, I can't say I do. Care to enlighten me?"

"Mars is my father."

"Oh, you're Italian? That explains the Latin on your walls, I guess."

He moves closer. "Lilith is my mother."

My smile withers. "Lilith?" Lilith is the Goddess of all succubi, the spiritual leader of my kind, if you will. "S-so, what does that make you?"

"Impervious to your abilities." He's toe to toe with me, a feral hunger in his eyes.

Gulp.

THE SUCCUBUS CHRONICLES

Chapter Three

Trouble and danger are plotting a gangbang, and I'm the main course. I am not liking how this is going, especially since he's having an effect on me. Parts of me are hardening; parts of me are softening. Blood is flooding my battle stations. If he's Lilith's son—I never knew she had a son—he thrives on sex as much as I do, craves it, takes it. He's not an incubus though. I've met a few of those fellows in my day, and they are a nasty bunch of rapists. No, Helveticus is made of subtler but far more deadly stuff. However, if Mars, the Roman god of war, is his father, all bets on a kinder, gentler Helveticus are off. Time to bluff.

"From where I'm standing, I think you want me as much as I want you. I think you—"

Demanding lips on mine seal my remaining words in my head while two brawny arms trap me in their embrace. His power and presence overwhelm me, my breath stolen to ransom for my submission, which I gladly yield. Lips move over mine, urging them apart so his tongue can tease, then invade my mouth.

We catch our breaths and begin the kiss anew. His agile tongue traces the edges of my teeth before curling in an embrace with my tongue. Tangy sweet flavors of dates and pomegranates tantalize me.

I'm pressed closer, my breasts flattening against the steely hard chest and abdomen. My arms slide up and lock around his neck, and a tiny whimper escapes. He cups my buttocks and pulls my hips to his.

"Perhaps I underestimated your abilities, succubus." A low growl precedes another kiss—long, slow, deep and toe curling. Molten desire sears my flesh, his touch the cause and the cure.

I lose all hope of winning this battle of sexual prowess; his masculine energy is so potent and compelling. My knees weaken, and my mind blanks out all thought other than how long before I can get his cock inside me, and why can't it already be now.

Now. Now. My hips rotate and grind against him, no longer under my control but under his. Between my legs a weeping emptiness yearns to be filled. The scent of my arousal betrays me, but so does his, creating a musky, complimentary blend of male and female.

Our fingers fumble with the knot holding my gown in place, the sash at his waist, the cloak on his shoulders. We aren't fast enough because our kisses slow our pace, and our bodies hinder our movements. Like two magnets, we cannot be parted, even to further the end goal. Could I be affecting him as strongly as he is affecting me? A thin current of triumph zings through me.

I nearly have his clothing ready to drop to the floor. "Where should we—"

I fly up in the air, in his arms. My clothing dangles precariously, as if it will fall from me any second, and when we reach his bedroom, it does. Other than my jewelry, I wear nothing but my skin and a thick coating of lust.

The bedroom is spacious and airy, the walls a dark masculine color. Furs cover his bed and the surrounding areas—the bedroom of a man who spends much time in it. Mine boasts similar comforts.

When he tosses me on his bed, I sink into the linens, crisp and sun-dried, the scent of the summer afternoon still present in their folds. I scramble to the center and lie on my back, my body laid out like a feast before him. He finishes removing the last of his clothes.

His gaze consumes me, dares me to look away. I cannot even if I wished.

I kick off my sandals as he kicks off his. I'm ready to drink in the sight of this magnificent male before me.

Skin burnished from the sun, taut muscles roping over his soaring frame, a dusting of hair on his chest and bisecting his abdominals, the same dark color as the curling locks cascading from his head—his beauty surpasses Apollo's. His strength matches Hercules'. His cock has no rivals, for it is of godlike proportions, long and thick and stands at full attention. The sizeable sac beneath is drawn upward and taut.

Helveticus takes hold of himself with a grip that brings out the muscles in his forearms, and pumps his fist up and down. A drop of pre-cum glistens on the tip when he tugs the foreskin down to reveal the plum-colored glans. I touch the tip of my tongue to my upper lip.

"You want this don't you, succubus?"

I nod. No point in being coy. I do want it, want him, more than any other I've ever beheld. I want him to shove his cock inside me to the root. I want him to flex and thrust those muscular hips to drive himself deep inside, to stroke and pet me from within. I want every inch of his succulent cock to fill my pussy, my mouth and my ass.

A sly smile accompanies him as he pounces on the bed, and like a large cat, crawls on his hands and knees toward me. When he reaches my calves, his hands blaze a trail for his tongue to follow, bathing my skin with liquid fire.

"Oh! Yes!" The words leap from my mouth. I try to hold my legs still but I need to move, to urge his tongue and his hands closer to where I need him most. "More!" My hips rock and rotate, coaxing him to spiral in to my pleasure's center.

"Mm, you taste good but I'll bet not as good as other parts of you." The soft hairs on his head brush against my inner thighs, teasing a moan from me.

My eyes drift shut and my head falls back and I feel—feel his roughened hands on my thighs, his hot mouth inching closer to my center, the silky sweep of his hair. "Helveticus, you are my undoing."

A low chuckle shakes the bed, but I am transported elsewhere when he reaches my labia. Contact is tentative at first, and I shy away, skittish but desperate at the same time. His tongue seeks my trembling flesh and reassures me with long lapping strokes. I nearly fly off the bed when he stabs deep inside me. How can a man's tongue be so long and adept at reaching all the way into my brain to lap up any remaining rational thought?

My cries come in soft mewls as he alternates laving my clit with plunging his talented tongue inside my pussy.

"Oh yes! Like that, right there, keep doing that!" I reach down and touch his head buried between my legs, threading my fingers into his hair. It's softer than I expected, thick and full. With light pressure, I pull him higher to torment my clit with more concentrated tongue-lashings. No more deep sea diving; I need him to wade in my shallows.

The threshold of my release looms closer when Helveticus moans into my channel, the vibrations against my clit nearly sending me over the edge. He plunges first one finger then a second inside me, while his lips and tongue nibble at the petals of my pussy, lapping the honey he finds there. His moan becomes a hum and I his instrument, vibrating with each note he plays on my sex.

My cries grow louder and echo in the massive room, and he laughs. His whole body shakes from his laughter, and the effect is devastatingly delicious.

I'm so close, so close, when suddenly he removes his mouth. A rush of air takes its place.

"No!" My hips rise up to follow his wonderful lips and tongue, to beg for more attention. He can't be done, he can't. He can't abandon me now!

Hands that held my thighs open slide up my hips then position themselves beside me on the bed. I open my eyes in time to see his head blot out my vision. As his mouth claims my mouth, his cock claims my pussy.

He is not gentle or slow, but rough and fast. Before I can catch my breath, he has impaled himself to the hilt. He doesn't move at first, just holds himself still and makes an animal-like sound, proclaiming his possession.

"Great Zeus, you undo me!" Slowly he pulls back then drives forward again. He repeats the move with exaggeration. "Fucking Olympus, so sweet, so tight." His balls bump against my ass with his next punishing thrust.

I open my thighs wider in welcome. Legs draw up and wrap around his back, eliciting a new groan from Helveticus.

"Fuck!" Two arms brace his upper torso in a raised position to allow him greater range of motion.

He nearly pulls out of me in a long fluid stroke, but his sizeable organ never completely leaves. The trip back inside my slick heat brings out my purr. His angle is perfect to tug at the covering to my pearl, a gentle massage that with each stroke nudges me closer to Elysium.

"Oh yes, more, more!" I cry out. My hips rock and strain for greater friction between male and female flesh.

Our gazes lock, and the corner of his mouth curls. He unleashes his inner beast and the real fucking begins. Like the lashes of whip, his plundering cock moves fast

and hard, striking sparks of desire like a knife on flint.
My wetness spills down into the crack of my ass as he
fucks me with a furious, unapologetic rhythm.

"You like that, succubus?"

"Yes!"

"I didn't hear you. What-did-you-say?" His hips
pound into mine.

"Yes-yes-yes-yes!" I time my words to each of his
plunges, with each of collision of our pelvises.

Helveticus lowers his torso to drape over mine.
His fingers dig into my hips to hold me still as he drives
himself inside me again and again. Breaths come in loud,
raspy pants.

No mercy. There is no mercy. He offers none, and
I'll not ask for it.

My traitorous pussy begs for the pounding to
cease, but I want more. I beg him to fuck me even harder.
The long slow climb to the heavens is nearly finished,
only the last few strokes, deeper, with grunting and other
lusty sounds coming from my lips and his.

Until all explodes with the violence of a volcano.
I fly out of myself as my body releases all its tension and
I crest the hill and begin my fall into oblivion.

A scream. His first, then mine. We are there
together, clinging one to the other, stealing every last
morsel of bliss our bodies can wrest from the other's,
until we land on the downy cushion of his bed.

He rests only a matter of minutes before he
mounts me yet again. The passion play repeats with even
more mind-numbing consequences.

The third time, though, I am sore and tell him so.
He doesn't care and takes me anyway. This climax is the
most powerful of all.

My pleas for mercy when he rouses for an
incredible fourth attack on my whimpering sex, he heeds,

but only as long as it takes to flip me to my stomach. Lying on top of me, the tip of his cock probes my ass, sliding between cheeks slick with his cum and my juices.

"I'm going to fuck your ripe, luscious ass now," he says. I bear down to open myself to him, to allow him to slowly push inside me inch by inch. When the hairs of his sex tickle my skin, he stops and we lie still. His weight is heavy on my back but not unbearably so.

As if he's read my thoughts, he rolls to his side, taking me with him, his massive staff still impaled in my ass. A thick finger finds my nub of pleasure and gives it a light flick as he flexes his hips and thrusts into me. Again he repeats the lazy flick and flex duo. On his third thrust, he dips his finger inside my pussy then pulls out of both my entrances.

"Why did you stop?" I ask, panting.

"I need something. Stay right there. Don't move."

The bed shifts and the air against my back chills from his absence. But soon he's back and his warmth reassures my skin.

"Lift your leg and let me enter you again," he says.

I comply, and he pushes through the tight, sensitive ring to reseat himself deep inside. It isn't his finger possessing my pussy, but a large, phallic shaped object, not quite as warm as he is, but hard and thick. I am filled to near bursting in both entrances.

"You like that? Being fucked in your cunt and ass at the same time?" He doesn't wait for my answer, but bites my earlobe and quickens the pace of both intruders he controls.

"More," I whisper. My eyes clamp shut as I ride the intense storm of ecstasy sweeping in to overwhelm me.

He gives me more—faster, harder, deeper and utterly ruthless.

"So fucking tight, gods be damned, you feel so fucking good."

I don't hear him anymore, because I am lost in the maelstrom of my climax. Whatever the hell he's fucking my pussy with is going in my suitcase when I'm packed off to Hades' lair. If I have to steal it, I will!

Helveticus grunts and furiously rams my ass until with a loud shout he surges forward a final time and stills, his organ pulsing and jetting his come, hot and copious. He pulls back with a soft groan and pushes forward in a final shuddering thrust, once again frozen as his vocalizations fade to silence.

I have never been with a man who possessed more stamina than me, but this one does. We have done nothing but transfer our sexual sustenance from one to the other, though he has left me weaker than I him.

How can such a man exist? Never have I been out performed in the bedroom before. Never.

I lift my arm, or try to lift it, but the thing barely acknowledges my command. My legs are similarly rebellious. Not good, and the fall of the shadows on his wall tell me I am still at his disposal for another hour. I don't think I will survive that long.

I steal a glance over my shoulder at my bedroom warrior. He dozes, thank the gods. He needs at least a little recovery time. Maybe I'll just shut my eyes for a bit too...

Chapter Four

Loud banging against a door in the distance awakens me. I am still weak but at least I can wiggle my toes. Curled around me from shoulders to ankles, his nose nestled into my hair, Helveticus is also waking.

"Damnation!" He jumps from the bed, with far too much energy for my liking, and with a sheet wrapped about his waist, hurries to answer the door.

While he's gone, I seek my clothing and sandals—no easy task, the room is in such disarray from our earlier frolicking. Strident voices from the next room halt me. I move closer to the bedroom door to indulge my curiosity.

"You've been here all this time? I've been looking all over for you! And why aren't you dressed already? Do you know what time it is? Don't you have any appreciation for what I've done for you?" The voice belongs to Tyche. My stomach does a free fall to my toes.

"I didn't ask you to do it. I never promised you any more than the one night." Helveticus's voice is raised and angry. "Leave me now so I can prepare for my battle!"

"Like pummeling that little wisp of a thing into a puddle of mead will even make you sweat. You could beat her with a cross word." A groaning sigh marks the close of her argument until she resumes her harangue, only this time in a much lower and deadlier tone. "Is there someone in your bedroom?"

"I don't answer to you. Please leave now," Helveticus says, his voice pitched in an equally dangerous range.

Eep! Tyche, can't find me here. Fortune giveth and she taketh away. I gather up my clothing and search for a place to hide.

"I think I'll just take a look!" Tyche's seething words foretell the opening of the door.

"No!" Helveticus yells. Scuffling, like sandals slipping on the tiles, grunts from exertion, and cries of frustration move closer.

From where I'm crouched behind a large shield in the corner, I can hear but cannot see.

"Let go of me. I know there's a woman in here! Where is she! Where's the whore you've been fucking!"

I make myself as small as possible, my muscles locked in a living rigor mortis.

The swish of fabric across the floor moves toward me. A deep male voice says, "There is no one here, Tyche. Once again your jealous imagination shames you. But even if there were, you have no right to challenge me like this!"

"No right? I just got you a ticket out of this place, lover! You don't think you owe me after what I did for you?" Tyche's snarling voice is close. She must be standing nearly toe-to-toe with Helveticus.

"You and I already settled our deal. I will not further subjugate myself to you. This duel is nothing but another scheme to re-enslave me, pitting me against a woman! You shame me! Are you hoping I'll bow out? Let my second clean up the messy details?"

Oh wow. He's livid. Tyche isn't one to piss off.

"Bah! I never took you for a coward, Helveticus."

"Why would you do this? What sort of machinations have you set into motion by choosing Willow?"

"Me? I had nothing to do with the succubus being chosen. That was wholly Aphrodite's affair. Though why she did it is anyone's guess."

The shuffle of sandals on the floor moves them further away. Their voices drop to inaudible levels. I wish

I could hear what Tyche's saying about Aphrodite, why she picked me, but I don't dare emerge from my hiding spot.

"Darling, don't be cross with me. It does not become you." An appeasing tone infuses her voice, now much closer.

"My apologies, my lady, but the shame of having to battle a female taints my tongue. It was badly done!"

He's afraid of her, that much I can tell even if I can't see his body language. My ears don't lie and my nose scents the spike in his anxiety.

Tyche laughs. "As to fighting a woman, think no more of it. Some say this Willow is actually a man, a shape-shifting incubus disguised to seduce whichever sex he chooses. Consider it. Do you think Aphrodite would take such a long-term interest in another woman? Though she likes to engage in love play with both sexes, she prefers cock to pussy. With Willow, can have her pick at any time."

A man? I am no man! How dare she say such about me!

Helveticus lets loose a throaty chuckle. "Then my lady best let me dress and prepare for my match. I appreciate your candor and will do my best to make you proud."

He's definitely afraid of her.

Feet shuffle across the floor and the door shuts with a soft thud. I peek out then emerge from my hiding spot and quickly don my robe.

When Helveticus does not immediately return, I glance at the window. A sheet of papyrus paper and a light gauzy cloth covers the opening. I'll fit, but it will be a tight squeeze. Giggles from the next room tell me he may not be back for a while, the man-slut.

I'm about halfway, having just wriggled and cajoled my breasts through, when I hear, "Oh, no you don't!" The voice's female owner seizes my legs and pulls. Hard.

Bracing my arms against the exterior wall gives me leverage. I am able to kick my feet to free them from my attacker. So long as she doesn't glimpse my face, I still have a chance. I wriggle forward and make a hair's breadth of progress only to be jerked backwards. My breasts are my last line of defense. If they go back through, so will I. Kicking no longer works because the grip on my legs is unyielding. I would swear they are Helveticus's hands, except they don't circle as much of my ankles as when he had me in that one weird but totally hot position earlier.

Arguing voices, both booming and screeching, continue inside the bedroom. I remain quiet, not wanting to attract the attention of passers-by who might rat me out for the tiniest of boons, especially from the goddess of chance.

Suddenly, the window enlarges to twice its normal size, and I'm plucked inside and tossed on my ass. How did that happen? I hastily tuck my breasts back inside my gown to correct the disrobing caused by the tug of war.

"The succubus! I knew it! Motherfucker! I knew you were lying."

"Tyche, calm yourself! Look what you did to my window! Any passing thief can rob me!" Helveticus says.

"I'll fix your damned window right after I curse this bitch who dares to touch what is mine!"

She raises her arms, her hair standing on its ends as she does. A gust of wind whistles in through the enlarged window opening, now door-sized. The wind grows fiercer as it whips around the bedroom, taking on a life of its own—a wind sprite. The sprite is probably another poor sucker who owes Tyche a favor.

"Stop it!" Helveticus yells over the roar. "Take your wrath out on me, not her. She is only here because I tricked her, to hedge my bet. I knew Aphrodite chose her for a reason. I was trying to discover what that reason was."

The wind sprite tries to blow up my gown, the pervert, but I slam down the fabric before he can lift it much higher than my knees.

"Hedge your bet? A second ago you were concerned about fighting a woman and blaming me! Now you say you knew all along Aphrodite rigged the lottery to choose this one. Are you playing me for a fool?"

You and me both, Tyche!

They stare at each other silently for a second. Tyche's eyes widen and her mouth falls open. "You double-dealing bastard! Tell me everything or the succubus dies!" In a softer, but far more menacing voice, she adds, "And you'll go into the arena against her second wearing my curse."

Helveticus glances my way and sighs. "Alright. I'll tell you. But let her go first. She's nothing more than the spoils of a deal with Aphrodite. She'll be dead, or wish she were, soon enough."

The breeze lessens in intensity as the sprite pulls himself into a tiny cyclone and makes a beeline for the bodice of my gown. His breath is like ice and my nipples harden. A soft chortle rumbles through the room as the sprite spins outside through the doorway Tyche made. I have never been a fan of the elementals.

Hands on her hips, Tyche locks her malevolent green eyes with mine. She jerks her head toward the door. "Get out! Now! Before I change my mind and curse you, too!"

I'm so confused. I don't understand Helveticus's plottings, but it sure seems like I'm going to come out the loser. Just when I thought he might actually be a nice guy.

I scramble to my feet and scurry home to suit up for battle. If I'm headed for the underworld, I don't want to be dead when I get there. The last thing I want is to be passed around amongst Hades' minions as soon as I arrive. That's how they treat soulless succubi in his domain.

    ***

Helios with his solar steeds and flaming chariot passes overhead on his daily trek to the west, signaling the start of the ceremonies. Drums beat out a primitive tattoo and incite the gathered crowd of nearly five thousand to stomp their feet in rhythm. The annual duel is the hottest event of the games, and people throw chariot-gate picnics and don the odd costumes to enhance the festivities. I would have been one of them, but this year I'm a combatant. This is what I've always wanted. I just wish my opponent wasn't nearly six and half feet tall, with biceps as thick as my thighs and a libido not only able to withstand my charms but to enslave them. I also wish I understood what plottings between Helveticus and Aphrodite were afoot.

Both Helveticus and I wear leather armor. We each possess a broad sword, a chain and a shield.

The announcer introduces each of us, prompting equally loud cheers. I focus on cobbling together whatever scraps of strategy I can find. I'm not a fighter; I'm a lover. I'm also not a quitter, and Hades, who hates pansy-types, will be watching

The trumpets signal the start of our match. We'll have ten minutes to battle before we'll be sent to neutral stations for the judging to occur if both fighters are still standing.

"Surrender and this will go much easier for you," Helveticus says as we square off.

"Why should I trust you? You've done nothing but lie to me since the beginning." I dash in swinging my sword at him but he easily parries my attempt and sends me flying to my knees.

"Because you can't beat me in a fight." He paces nearby but doesn't attack, despite the heckling from the crowd. "You're welcome, by the way."

I scramble to my feet in time to avoid the downward stab his sword, which would have missed me anyway. What sort of theatrics is he playing at?

"I'm welcome for what?" I ask.

"For saving your ass from Tyche."

I blow out a puff of audible disbelief. "Seemed more like you were saving your own ass, long enough to fight a girl for your freedom. Arrogant coward! I won't be beaten so easily!"

We continue to circle each other. The crowd's whistles and boos grow louder.

Helveticus roars and tosses his sword to the ground, mocking my ability to challenge him. The crowd laughs, stoking my ire.

"I was going to be chosen no matter what ticket I held. Tyche promised me that," he says. A second later, he rushes to tackle me, but I deftly sidestep him, and he stumbles. Talk about bad acting. He quickly regains his feet, a sneer on his lips. "Aphrodite chose you because someone persuaded her."

"Persuaded her? How did you do that? Did you sleep with her?" Sensing he's momentarily distracted by his confession, I charge in with my sword. He grabs a

handful of dirt and tosses it into my face, blinding me
enough to foil my aim.

"Actually, I didn't." He dives and seizes his chain
and shield. "I'm not that kind of guy. Someone else
convinced Aphrodite she could settle her debt to you for
landing you in this place *and* offer you as a concubine to
curry favor with Hades. Win-win for her."

"And for you!" I bite out as I swing my sword in a
wide arc toward his midsection. He deflects the blow
with his shield. "But I'll play along. If you didn't
convince her to choose me, who did?"

He snorts and begins to whirl his chain over his
head. "Who would gain from your absence? Who wants
more than anything else to be the most beautiful creature
in Sisyphus Prison? Who pushed you into my path?"

An invisible hand grips my throat and heart and
squeezes. "Narcissus?"

Chapter Five

"Narcissus made a deal with Aphrodite to get rid of me?" I choke out.

"It had to be him. He somehow knew Tyche had already promised me one of the spots—"

"Tyche's sister, Nemesis, told him!" Narcissus's end game starts to take on greater clarity. "He deliberately pitted me against you? I can't believe he'd do that to me!"

"Why do you think he sent you over to swap tickets with me? He knew I'd be chosen no matter what." Helveticus lowers his arm, the spinning arc out to his side.

I wrack my brain but the betrayal is too raw, too fresh, and Helveticus is still swinging that damned chain. "I don't know!"

"He thought he was giving you a chance to beat me, by seducing me, by draining me. That is what you had planned, right?"

The grip on my throat loosens, and I take a shaky breath. "Narce thought he was helping me?"

He nods and swings the chain at me, but misses by a wide margin. The crowd boos, obviously not fooled by his lame attempt.

"I doubt he had much trouble convincing Aphrodite of his scheme," he says, increasing the speed of his whirling weapon.

Helveticus and I circle each other warily. I suppose he's comfortable telling me all this because he has the upper hand when it comes to physical combat. The advantage Narce thought I had disappeared the moment Helveticus told me who he was, who his mother was.

"I don't want to go to the underworld, to Hades." My voice is small and shaky. I don't want to lose my composure. If I do, I might as well lay down all my weapons and swap one prison for another: the devil I know for the devil I don't.

"It's better than here," he says. "Surrender and you can negotiate a deal like Demeter did for Persephone, go above ground for a few months every year. Hades will only want a few souls in return. Isn't that what you did before you came here, anyway? Collected souls for him in exchange for sex with their mortal owners?"

"Yes and no. I worked for one of his underlings." I suppose Hades might be open to a bit of negotiation. I always did love my job before losing it once I landed in Sisyphus.

Just as I've almost rationalized my loss, Helveticus releases his chain in a wide-sweeping arc near my legs. Though his aim is low and I jump in time to avoid the brunt of the impact, my heel suffers a graze. The crowd cheers my maneuver and begins a clapping, chanting cry. I'd be happier if my foot didn't smart like a Promethean liver at sunset. *Damn him!* He needs to at least hurt a little before I give up.

"Are you done playing?" His helmet mostly hides his face but not enough to hide the thin line his lips form.

"Not until I've beaten you."

When our circling continues too long, the crowd again voices its disapproval.

"If one of us does not draw blood soon, they'll send in our seconds. Have you seen mine?" he asks.

I haven't. I don't even know who my second is. I'm sure they introduced us, but my head apparently did not register his identity or his fighting abilities.

Helveticus charges. I throw up my shield and ready my sword, a useless move because he barrels into me, knocking me to the ground. I lose my grip on my sword when I'm hit. Tossing his shield and chain aside, he dives forward and pins me down, manacling both of my wrists above my head.

"Signal your surrender and stop playing around! It's a good plan, better than rotting in this place! I'll even help you negotiate." His face is close to mine, the lushness of his mouth a sensuous counterpart to the masculine planes of brow and cheeks.

"Why would you do that?" An irrational urge to kiss away the tenseness in his stubborn jaw fights its way past my preservation instincts. I shift beneath him.

The movement provokes a small smile. He's mocking me. The bastard is erect and poking me with his male weaponry. He might be Lilith's son and have a way with women, but two can play at that game. I blast a mega dose of pheromones his way and struggle to free myself. His arousal hardens and grows. *Good!*

"Do not bring your sex tricks into this battle, Willow. You want to incite me into raping you in front of this crowd?" He snarls his words at me, our helmets bumping at the foreheads.

"It's not rape if I orchestrate it." I squirm and undulate beneath him.

His breath hitches and his hips slowly grind against mine. "Maybe the crowd expects it."

"Maybe they do," I spit out, hoping he takes my challenge, hoping the observers and judges realize I'm a succubus and can wield sex as a soldier wields a knife.

The crowd roars louder, savage and bloodthirsty.

We stare at each other.

He releases my hands, and pressing his full weight on me, he rips off his helmet and throws it down. I mimic his movement.

I can't make out the spectators' chants at first until a smile curls Helveticus's lips into an archer's bow, taut with merriment at my expense.

"Choose your method of defeat. Either way, I will impale you, but remember, Hades is watching." A snicker escapes those lips, and his tongue slips out to wet them.

The words are clear now. "Fuck-her, fuck-her, fuck-her!"

Do I want Hades to see what I can do or not? "I..." I can't think, damn him! He's fogged my brain with his scent, but I've driven him to this point. "I don't—"

He makes the decision for me and rips the hem of my short gown away from me. The linens I've wrapped around my hips, he tears through as if no more substantial than a spider's web.

My impetuous hands drop and fumble with the loincloth he wears beneath his tunic. The heat of his cock draws my hand to seize it in a tight grip. Wetness floods the space between my legs. *Gods help me, I want him, it. Here. Now.*

"Let me inside you," he rasps. He's offering me the choice, not using his superior strength against me, strength that could easily take versus receive.

"Who wins if I do?" I'm honestly not sure, but my legs part and make space, hips angling up to receive him. My body has apparently chosen for me. *Traitor!*

He positions the head of his cock at my entrance and pauses. The chanting grows louder. Helveticus gives an answering shout and shoves forward. He starts thrusting and grunting like a lust-crazed brute, all rough and filthy, and I love it.

But I don't want to be on my back, rutting in the dirt. With new found strength, I roll him off me. He slips out but pulls me on top, my legs astride his hips. I rise and nestle the head of his cock between my pussy lips.

With a glorious battle cry, I descend, bottoming out with his thick length stretching and filling me. Two can play at his game. Undulating motions take over. The crowd's chants change to "Fuck-him, fuck-him, fuck-him!"

Helveticus grips my hips and moves beneath me, meeting me thrust for thrust. "Surrender," he growls, and I want to laugh.

"You surrender!" I increase the pace of my movements and watch his eyes roll back in their sockets.

He says no more; his breath comes too quickly to afford him that luxury.

I plant my hands on his chest and ride him, my mighty stallion. His fingers flex and release, and the muscles in his neck grow taut. Every part of him tenses. The veins in his neck bulge and his skin flushes. He's close.

"Ah, ah fuuu-uck!" He thrusts upward, nearly unseating me as he bows his back off the ground, shuddering as he comes.

But I'm not finished with him yet. I continue to work his turgid length seeking my own climax. I show him no mercy just as he showed me no mercy earlier in his bed.

Faster I move, my moans turning into breathy pants. He feels so fucking good. Whether due to him or the presence of an audience, no sexual encounter has ever, in my life been so charged with anticipation.

I ride his shaft, which amazingly has not softened a lick. His cum seeps out and lubricates my path further. I press forward, grasping his shoulders. The tingly friction is unraveling my sanity one thread at a time. I'm frantic and furious in my fucking, and in a distant part of my mind the claps and shouts egg me on, not that I need them. Nearly ready to explode I rise and fall, once, twice, thrice. His fingers dig into the flesh of my thighs as I breach my boundaries and rip a perfect pleasure from him. A piercing cry explodes from my lungs. Everyone quiets until there is only my voice rising into the arena as millions of stars explode in my head and course through my veins. Spent, I collapse onto Helveticus's chest, snatching ragged breaths of air.

"I declare Helveticus the victor!" Tyche announces.

The spectators, however, are not pleased with her hasty decision, and dissension sweeps like a plague of locusts through their ranks.

"No, the female, Willow wins!" some cry.

"No, he took her! Helveticus wins!" cry others.

Battling voices grow louder and more dissonant.

I climb off Helveticus and extend a hand to help him rise to his feet. With a resigned grin he accepts it. "Congratulations, I think your victory is nigh," he says.

I shake my head. "No, you will prevail."

The bolt of lightning and clap of thunder silences the crowd where the admonishments of Tyche failed.

Over Helveticus's shoulder, near the gods' spectator boxes, Zeus rises from his seat. I hadn't even known he'd be here today. He stands between Aphrodite and Tyche who have locked into a fighting stance, their fingers tangled in one another's hair. He parts them and steps forward as if to address the crowd. Hades is nowhere to be seen, the slacker.

Zeus doesn't speak but applauds. Soon the rest of the spectators join in with their clapping and stomping.

"Well done, Helveticus," he says.

Great. The boys always stick together.

His attention shifts to me, and I prepare to be officially dubbed the loser. "Well done, Willow." He motions with his hands for quiet. "I, Zeus, declare the match a draw!" Cheers erupt until he motions for quiet again. "Since both are victors, both will be freed from Sisyphus and granted immunity from retaliation by either goddess or her acolytes." He glances first at Tyche then at Aphrodite. "However, since both Helveticus and Willow are also losers, they will be banished to the remote island of Spanos until they can learn to play nicely together." Zeus throws a wink and a smile to Helveticus and me.

I glance at Helveticus to gauge his reaction to this rather unorthodox turn of events. The side of his mouth hitches up ever so slightly. His eyes shift into their corners to meet mine. "Your ass is mine now, Willow," he says under his breath.

"As if, fighter boy," I mutter back. "Better fortify your energy reserves." I spin to face him dead on. "Because you're going to need them."

"Bring it!" he says, then laughs.

I try to project a stoic demeanor, but I can't maintain it. I too burst out laughing, and with our arms around each other, we stroll toward the arena's exit and take our first steps out of Sisyphus.

THE SUCCUBUS CHRONICLES

DEDICATION

To all the real men who make BOBs totally
Dunnecessary.

THE SUCCUBUS CHRONICLES

SUCCUBUS STEAM

Lila Shaw

Copyright © 2013

Sexual energy comes in more than one form, and many have attempted the manufacture of a counterfeit source. If an intrepid succubus were to become a free agent, with none to demand tribute from her, she might possibly craft a man-like substitute. I have never heard of nor would I personally make such choice, for I am the first succubus and have a duty to my kind. However, I have lived long enough to know that the moment anyone says something is impossible, someone will eventually prove him wrong.

—Miss Lilith's Guide to the Care and Keeping of a Succubus

Chapter One

"Damnation!"

Why is a suitable spanner never handy when I need one? It's my own fault I suppose. Perhaps if I put my tools away after using them, I wouldn't so often find myself in a rage of futility. However, my computations did show that time spent putting tools away exceeded the periodic time spent hunting.

I search the vicinity of my creation and find what I seek right where I left it, protruding from the socket that will later house the aural reception and processing unit, the very heart and soul of my months of labor.

"Let's see how this latest tweak to your settings has you functioning, my dear." I speak to it, him, but realize from his silence that I've forgotten to re-engage the perpetual self-winding gears.

With a buzz then a tiny jolt, it stirs. Adam. My creation. His eyes flutter open. The pupils dilate and block out the red light glowing behind the lenses. He senses me. "Good morning, Violet," he says, rising to a sitting position. Legs dangling off the edge of the table, he peruses me. "I adore you in lavender."

I glance down at my attire and am greeted with shades of pink and ivory. Adam's color rods will need further tweaking, but I'm much closer. He used to see only shades of grey, black and white.

"Good morning, Adam. Did you sleep well?"

He cocks his head. He should be able to answer my question, though he has no concept of sleep. The response I trained him to give is drawn from one of three possibilities: "I did, thank you", "Passably", and—

"Alas, it was a challenge." The third option.

I provide my usual response of, "I'm very sorry to hear that, Adam. I hope we will be able to set you to rights soon."

"I look forward to it." His voice gives me a momentary shudder. I must confess to having stolen the timbre and cadence from a certain male of my acquaintance. Though I am estranged from the man, I do still love the voice, so much that I *gifted* it to Adam.

Our usual morning volley of conversation concluded, Adam sits quietly and stares blankly into the distance. I suppose I should teach him a few fidgets or tics if only to make him seem more human, though he is an amazing automaton. To say I am proud of my work is a gross understatement. Coming into the knowledge and experience to build a machine such as Adam hasn't always been easy.

"Adam, let's try a few diagnostics today, shall we?"

"As you wish."

"Raise your right leg, please."

Adam executes my command flawlessly.

"Very good, Adam. Lower your right leg and raise your left leg."

Again he complies. I take him through a well-established routine and check a few new motions I've added. He performs all exactly as I expect, and my expectations are very high. They have to be. Given my own nature, I require an exquisite amount of finesse and complete discretion. If all goes well, Adam will be my lover.

The double-edged sword of being the product of a succubus mother and a mortal father is that while I am not a predator and can be satisfied, for a time, through self-administered sexual release, Society does not look kindly upon a wanton. A succubus half-breed, such as myself, who hobnobs with the highest echelons of London society, is bride in a difficult marriage of extremes. Any act that wants of propriety, and I would find myself ushered out on the first coach to the wilds of Cornwall. My half-sisters dwell there to feed upon the thick abundance of sailors passing through her ports. Yet, because my lifespan is finite, I do prefer the company of mortals to those who prey upon them, even if I must periodically engage in discreet acts of congress. My full-blooded succubus sisters are preternatural, but they are parasitic to mortals as are their loathsome incubus fathers and cousins.

If I could but keep a man enslaved in secret within the bowels of my home, I might achieve the same end. But I abhor slavery of any kind. An automaton, however, offers the unlimited, on-demand joys of the male sex, with the added benefit of complete discretion. He will be silent unless I permit him to speak, still unless I power his inner workings, and he will never speak cruelly or in a condescending manner to me.

My superb design has yielded iron and aluminum workings, covered by a material so identical to human flesh, it fools even my own discerning senses of sight, smell, taste and touch.

My Adam is nearly complete. I've stitched hair onto his head, my own as chance would have it, and onto his sex, his chest and arms. I even added a dash to his upper lip because I do adore kissing a mustachioed man, perhaps because it adds an air of danger without invoking true peril.

Adam's limbs are long and powerful, sculpted in the manner of Michelangelo's David. His face is rugged yet symmetrical, with sculpted cheekbones and jawline, but with full, fleshy lips and a dangerously provocative cleft in his chin.

I've reserved my best efforts in the design and function of his manhood. After all, that is his primary purpose: to sate my appetite upon demand, one that is both carnal and life sustaining. His cock is nearly the thickness of my wrist and the length of my foot and is fixed in a permanent state of readiness. He wears no clothing but the smile I affixed upon his handsome visage. He need not suffer any embarrassment over his nude and aroused state. He has nowhere to go and is happy–as much as an automaton can be– to forever remain at his station in my laboratory with its adjoining bedchamber.

Soon, I will be able to shed the yoke of this cloaked life, once Adam is ready.

My butler, Barrick, alerts me by way of a volley of signals that cascade into my laboratory far below street level. The end result is a reproduction of Barrick's voice down to the last inflection in tone that alerts me to the arrival of my guests, thirty minutes prior to what had been arranged.

I do not enjoy the company of my half- sisters, yet they insist on making periodic visits to my London home. They are coarse and unpredictable and threaten my already precarious social standing.

"Why are they always early when I wish they were late and late when I wish they were early!" I proclaim.

"I do not know, Violet. Shall we discuss it further?" Adam says.

"That was a rhetorical question, Adam. There is no logical answer other than capriciousness."

"Capriciousness," he says, swirling the word around in his mouth. He tilts his head and makes eye contact. "Explain capriciousness."

"Capriciousness means unpredictable, subject to whims, or in my sisters' cases, behavior intended solely to disconcert." I smile at his inquisitiveness and ability to increase his intelligence. I had intended a certain amount of growth in his mental faculties, but his enthusiastic expansion of such has surpassed even my dreams.

I disengage Adam's gears with a sigh and place a kiss of hope upon his cheek.

The trip to my parlor I make at a leisurely pace. My sisters must be taught that I do not make haste to reward their ill-time arrival. Once settled, I give a nod to Barrick to admit my guests.

"Violet!" Morganna sweeps into my parlor, unfurling her scarf and unbuttoning her coat as she covers the distance between us.

"Thank you, Barrick," I say. Morganna's confidence that Barrick will catch and tend to her discarded items mortifies me. Barrick has always been a noble and faithful servant and does not deserve such haughty presumptiveness. "Would you bring us some tea, please?"

"Certainly, my lady and perhaps some of Cook's tea cakes as well." Barrick gives a shallow bow but not before I catch the lift of his sardonic brows.

Morganna spins as if she's only now realizing a male is in the room. Unusual for her. Her lips purse and her eyes make a lazy perusal of Barrick's retreating backside. "Your butler is a male masterpiece. You always engage and somehow manage to retain the most pleasing servants. Wherever do you find them?"

I embrace her and place a kiss upon each cheek. "Do you really care?"

Morganna rolls her eyes and drops into a brocade chair near the window. "How are you, my dear?"

I take the chair opposite and arrange my skirts to stall whilst I decide upon the best answer. "Well. I am well." Short and simple rarely works but is always worth a try.

"Lyle says you've been hiding out of late, keeping your appearances in Society to the barest minimum. Why so, dear sister?"

And this is the main reason I do not like my sisters to visit. They attract unsavory types of creatures, in Morganna's case, an incubus named Lyle. I am usually able to avoid him, but when my sisters visit, I cannot prevent him from calling upon them, nor they from inviting him.

"I've been quite busy tending to Great Uncle Malcolm's affairs. Where is Demelza, by the way? She did accompany you did she not?"

"She did. She is at Lyle's. I suspect they are ... entertaining one another." Morganna presses a demure hand to her mouth, mocking the scandal that would ensue if the 'ton knew the type of entertaining my sisters preferred.

I stroll to my rolltop desk—eager to change the subject and hasten Morganna's departure—and withdraw an envelope. "Here is what you came for."

A few strides and Morganna is before me, her hand extended. "How much?"

"Five hundred thousand each for you and Demelza," I say, referring to the size of her share of our great uncle's liquid assets. As per his will, my two half-sisters are to receive forty percent each of his liquid assets to my twenty, but I receive all his other assets.

"Pity the old codger short-changed you, Violet. Considering you were always his favorite, I find that rather odd. This house cannot possibly be worth the difference in our inheritances." She tuts and tucks the money into the bodice of her gown.

I tut as well for neither Morganna nor Demelza has ever understood my regard for our great uncle. To my great relief, they are also ignorant of his laboratory. That alone is worth the difference and more in our cash inheritances.

The discovery that my great uncle was not only an inventor, but also a master of automatons, ranked among the happiest moments of my life. He did at first question why one of my fair sex should find clockwork and steam-powered beings so fascinating. As I demonstrated my keen interest, not only in observing him in action, but in eventually surpassing his skill, he declared me his favorite niece. His death brought both crushing grief and great riches that included his well-appointed laboratory in the heart of London. That a comfortable abode lay above it in the quaint district of Mayfair has been an added bonus.

"Lyle sends his best, by the way," she says, flashing a knowing grin bracketed by a pair of disarming dimples.

"I do not see why you two court that blackguard."

"Ah, sister, you have obviously not been the beneficiary of his considerable talents in the boudoir." She paces to the window and gazes out into the darkness cloaking the street. "You intrigue him, you know, by refusing to receive him. What man, mortal or otherwise, can resist a chase? You have only to let him catch you if you truly wish to be rid of him."

I doubt that. "No, thank you. I don't have time to play his games anyway."

Morganna spins back around. "Pish. You two used to be friendly. So sad you had a falling out." She retakes her chair. "Whatever caused it, tis a pity, because Lyle is quite," she draws in a deep breath, "extraordinary!"

I cannot deny the kernel of truth in her words. Lyle is extraordinary—tall and handsome as the devil's best with a velvet tongue capable of talking his way in between a nun's thighs. Unknown to my sisters, Lyle and I have a mutual history. I must confess to having experienced a momentary lapse in judgment that acquainted me with another of his tongue's talents. It also acquainted me with the hazardous nature of his particular brand of supernatural attention. The problem with having carnal relations with an incubus is he siphons off whatever sustenance I gain, rendering our coupling both fruitless and risky if he takes more than he gives. In Lyle's case, our one encounter left me in an energy deficit for which I've never fully forgiven him.

"You forget I am not like you and Demelza. I do not have your... stamina."

A soft knock on the door heralds Barrick's return with a tea service and some of Cook's finest cakes. He artfully arranges the tray and cups, rises and announces, "Miss Demelza and Mr. Lyle have just arrived. Shall I usher them in, Mistress?"

Morganna claps her hands. "Oh, they made it after all! Yes, yes, Barrick, please do have them join us."

My mouth opens to protest but before I can do so, Demelza sweeps in. "Violet! My darling little sister." She pulls me into an embrace and buries her nose in my hair. When she pulls back, her nose is wrinkled in disgust. "Phew! What have you been into?" She takes another sniff. "You smell of grease and," another sniff, "coal."

"Always a joy to see you, too, sister," I say, with a hard edge to my voice.

A fit of laughter escapes her. She draws Lyle over, still laughing. "Lyle. She hasn't changed a bit as you can tell."

Lyle cocks his head to one side and studies me, raking his gaze from hips to hair to bosom, where he lingers inappropriately before meeting my eyes. "She's still as beautiful as ever." That voice, Adam's voice, is like a fine brandy on a cold winter's night—mellow, seductive, but with a slight bite. "Violet." He takes my hand and presses a scorching kiss upon my knuckles. A frisson of lust courses from that tiniest point of contact straight to my sex. My knees buckle slightly from the potency of his effect on me.

Demelza slaps him on the shoulder with the glove she's peeled off. "No, silly goose, not her appearance, her tart tongue."

Lyle says nothing but smiles slyly at me. *Mother Lilith, please help me!* I pull my hand back and point to the available seating for my late arrivals, indicating for Lyle to take the one farthest from me, not that it's a safe enough distance to spare my sanity.

"What have you been up to lately, Violet?" Lyle purrs, pouring himself some tea. He really has no manners at all, and it's not because he doesn't know better. I'm convinced he does it solely to unnerve me.

"A bit of scientific observation, a few field trips, the usual." My nefarious plan is to bore him into dropping this particular line of inquiry. "The London museum currently has the most delightful exhibit of flying ships, all steam-powered and beautifully rendered in brass and brightly hued canvas. The propellers alone are works of art—brilliant amalgamations of science and artistry. It's quite fascinating. I'm hoping to stowaway on one someday soon." I can't help but titter at my confession because it's true.

Far from being bored like my sisters, however, Lyle perks up at my mention of flying ships. "Have you read about The *Icarus*? She is taking passengers as far north as Scotland, west to Ireland and east to Paris."

"The *Icarus*? No, I haven't."

"Sister, please do not get him started on The *Icarus* or you'll never shut him up," Demelza pleads, her mouth full of cake.

Lyle grins, his teeth on display like a strand of perfectly matched pearls. "Yes. If one has sufficient disposable income, passage can easily be secured. I myself have enjoyed her ride at least twice. Once is never enough. Sailing through the clouds high above the rabble of humanity is a thrill few other experiences can surpass." I'm shocked to note that despite his lascivious nature, Lyle is genuinely keen on something other than sex for a change. "Of course, in a few short weeks, I shall have my very own flying machine. You are more than welcome to fly with me, my dear. I can lift your spirits in more ways than one!" And there it is, back again. Infuriating man!

We drink our tea and make idle chitchat, during the whole of which my mind wanders to Adam. I cannot help it with his aural sire sitting directly across from me. When Morganna announces she is sufficiently stuffed and bored (and her money safely stowed) she stands to leave. Demelza follows suit. Lyle does not.

"Charming hostess as always, Violet, but I must be getting on." Morganna reaches for and pulls the cord that launches a series of cogs and wheels. She smiles as the tones of a bell can be heard in a far away part of the house. "Uncle Malcolm always had the most delicious inventions."

Within seconds, Barrick enters. I ask him to fetch their coats and rouse their carriage drivers so my visitors can, at last, take their leave.

Finally, Lyle stands, after my sisters are securely wrapped in their coats. He strolls to my side and gently presses his hand against the small of my back. The contact feels far too intimate, far too suggestive of other pleasures that tempt, oh yes they tempt, with a ferocity only an incubus can elicit. I clench my fists to hold my physical reaction in check.

"Do let me know if you wish to fly with me. I would greatly enjoy your stimulating company," he says in a voice so low and lazy none but me can have heard it. Despite my efforts, I tremble and lean into his hand.

Lyle's arrogant smirk claims a victory I've failed to deny him. Insufferable beast!

Chapter Two

Lyle visits me twice more over the next two weeks. He comes first with my sisters. We partake of an evening meal together before my visitors flit off for an orgy with a theatre troupe.

During his second, uninvited visit, I catch him prowling around my basement when I return early from high tea with the ladies Smythe and Goulding. The man has the audacity to quiz me about what I've hidden behind the doors, which I keep locked to deter overly curious servants and unwelcome visitors with prying eyes. He devises some flimsy excuse about having misunderstood the date of my invitation for a second dinner my sisters' wrangled over my protests. Finding no one at home to answer the bell—a lie—he admitted himself, claiming to be concerned about my welfare.

After that, the frequency with which Lyle's and my paths cross escalates. The rate is too shocking to be accidental. The man is stalking me. Perhaps I should sleep with him once more so he'll move on to his next conquest, but I'm too busy and can't afford to spend an entire day or more in bed recovering my strength.

***

Today I seek a form of aloe gel to apply to Adam's artificial skin. Chelsea is my usual destination for such an item and indeed I am successful in finding what I need within my first half hour. Turning the corner, I run straight into the hard wall of a man's chest.

"My apologies, sir, I—" The words catch in my throat as the familiar tug and tingle of a potent sex magic grips me. The man's familiar scent wafts into my nostrils—pure sex and desire. No, no, no. "Lyle. What are you doing here? Are you following me?"

"Following you? I think not. I was merely doing a bit of, uh shopping." His hand is on my arm, preventing me from escaping him without attracting undue attention.

"Right. What could you possibly want in Chelsea?"

Surprisingly, he reaches inside a bag I hadn't noticed before and withdraws a nosegay of violets that he presents to me. "Exactly the person I purchased these for. They reminded me of you...Violet."

"What do you want, Lyle?"

"Why do you assume I want anything?" He smiles down at me.

I cock my head to the side in wry disbelief that he would deny having any premeditated designs on me.

"Very well. I never could fool you, could I?" He releases my arm, and I shake my head. "Your sisters are of the opinion that you are hiding something of great value to which they believe they might have a claim. I agreed to help them discover if their suspicions were true." He takes a step closer and leans his head down to mine. "Since you are quite susceptible to my wiles."

"What makes you think I'm up to anything? And I'm not that susceptible. I am more than capable of refusing you."

He moves his lips to my ear and whispers, "Not if I willed otherwise." The warmth of his breath triggers a wave of heat through my body like the first flames to kindling. Pulling back, he adds, "But I am a believer in free will. As to the other topic, ever since your great uncle died, you've practically become a hermit in that stuffy old house of his. It's not healthy, Violet, especially for one such as yourself."

"One such as myself?"

"Half mortal." He takes my hand and draws it through the crook of his arm and we start walking, or rather he propels us both forward. To the casual observer, we are a man and a woman on a leisurely stroll through the vendor stalls of the Chelsea market.

"Why do you care, Lyle? What am I to you? Have my sisters offered you remuneration if I am discovered to be sitting on a pirate's booty within the bowels of my uncle's home?"

Lyle gives a soft snort and shoots me a sideways glance. "Contrary to what you may think, I do care about you, Violet. I am your most ardent admirer."

"I am nothing but a challenge to you, a conquest to be mounted like a stag on a wall. If you weren't a danger to my well-being, I'd have surrendered to you if only to set you on your merry way to your next trophy."

"You wound me with your base assassination of my character."

I stop short and stare up into his eyes, a deceptively benign shade of emerald. "You're an incubus, Lyle. You can't help what you are any more than a wolf can help its hunger for a sheep. But you still haven't answered my question about my sisters. Why are you helping them? What have they offered you?"

"Ah, my dear. You have it backwards; it is they who are helping me. You and I both know there are no treasures in your uncle's home those two would find of any value. I had only to plant the seed that there might be to bring them to London and in turn have them bring me to you." He releases my arm, tips his hat and bows. "Good day, dear Violet. I'm sure we shall meet again soon." And with that, he melts into the crowd and is gone.

THE SUCCUBUS CHRONICLES

Chapter Three

A week passes and Adam is finally ready for his maiden voyage, the one that will end his virginity, if such can be bestowed on an automaton.

"How are you this evening, Adam?" I wind his gears and add a brick of coal to his inner burners. Even and steady warmth to the touch is a critical design element I have taken great pains to perfect.

But my greatest source of pride lies in Adam's ability to converse and express intense satisfaction. I do adore vocal encouragement. His moans, groans, grunts, pants and shouts of pleasure are programmed to randomly erupt upon the stimulation of certain trigger points. I have also bestowed him with the ability to learn from the feedback I offer. In short, the more time I spend with Adam, the more I will enjoy him. For his part, there is no displeasing Adam. Ever.

"Adam?"

"Yes, Madam?"

"I am desirous of your copulatory skills. My itch requires release and my body its nourishment."

"As you wish, my love," he says. When in pleasure mode, he no longer refers to me as Madam but as My Love, a finer touch that pleases me highly.

He moves toward me, his steps catlike in their grace and silence. I watch with both the proud eye of his maker and the lustful eye of his lover.

Into his open arms I move, and he envelops me. His coal furnace clicks along nicely with the rhythm of a human heartbeat as his skin warms mine, neither too hot nor too cool—perfect. His full, sensuous mouth descends for a kiss. He feels exactly as a man should—hard and powerful, yet with a gentle touch in the press of his palms against my sides. His lips apply pressure to my lips, his artificial tongue, flavored with peppermint and chocolate, sweeps against my own.

I pull back to offer verbal encouragement. This I enjoy, because the more we interact, the more superb his lovemaking skills. "An excellent kiss, Adam. Do it again only, this time, swirl your tongue with mine then run it along the inside of my teeth. The kiss may then travel to my jaw, ear and neck, especially my neck."

Adam executes my commands with thrilling results. His tongue sweeps and dips and lays tracks of desire that end at the hollow of my throat. I feel the tightening of his arms about me and arch back to give him greater access to my erogenous zones.

"Continue on the other side," I prompt.

He does, finally returning to his home base at my lips for a kiss that ratchets my own internal combustion engine into a higher gear. Heat courses through me and liquid desire pools in my sex. My scalp, fingers and toes tingle. Part of me wants to command him to take me, release me, feed me, but slow and steady must be our game plan as I train him.

When my knees are nearly jellified from his interactive kissing instruction, I whisper my next command in his ear. "Undress me, slowly, paying homage to my body as you reveal it."

"Oh yes, my love," he says in a mimicking whisper.

Nimble fingers, themselves works of art that my great uncle would admire were he still alive, untie and loosen the laces of my dress. It puddles to the floor at my feet, leaving me in my corset and bloomers.

"Over on the bed." His forceful demand surprises me. I don't remember adding that command to his repertoire. The serendipitous thrill sends a frisson of pleasure through me as I move to my bed.

I lie back upon the immaculate bedclothes and gaze at my creation. He is gloriously nude, a work of erotic art to rival even the great Da Vinci. His erection bobs as he saunters lazily toward me, his eyes scanning my remaining garments. He should be computing the means for disrobing me, face fiercely determined, but instead he smiles. Another niggle of astonished pride courses through me.

He rolls me over onto my stomach, his weight upon my thighs as he straddles me. The laces whip at lightning speed from their eyelets and soon the corset loosens, and then falls to either side.

A tickle of hair (his mustache?) grazes my back between my shoulder blades before his lips brand me with their heat. His hands hold either side of my torso, thumbs sweeping in a semi-circular motion. My skin rouses to his touch. He slides those hands down, down, down until they slip beneath to untie the drawstring at my belly. The fabric loosens enough to slide down over my hips, but there is no quickening to his pace, no matter how much I squirm beneath him. The hands retrace their paths to either side of my hips then around to cup the flesh of my buttocks.

A groan rumbles against my back. I don't remember that being part of his lesson plan either. Perhaps I accidentally brushed one of his trigger spots?

"My love, you are exquisite."

That, I did teach him. The delivery in his bass register brings a purr to my lips.

He draws off my pantaloons and I am clothed only by the warmth of his hands and the soft press of his mouth. His mustache tickles my thighs, the backs of my knees and calves.

"Adam, that is both heavenly and maddening at the same time. Are you registering all my responses?"

"Oh, aye, my love, aye." More soft kisses. "Shall I bestow the same pleasures upon the flip side of your body?"

"Oh, aye, Adam, aye." I adore his hushed word choices and repeating them will lock them in his memory for future use.

He picks me up and, with a random spark of sauciness I hadn't expected, tosses me onto my back. His body covers mine, his weight propped up on his elbows that rest by my shoulders. A kiss, a gentle bite on my chin and he lifts up and slides down.

I present my breasts to him, but he pushes back onto his haunches and stares.

"Oh no," I murmur. "Please don't let his clockworks have wound down. Not now. Not yet." I raise up on my elbows, ready to pop open his inner workings panel when I notice a flicker in his eyes.

"Beautiful," he whispers before he takes my offerings in each of his hands.

I fall back with a small squeal of happiness. His dark head drops to my right breast where his tongue flicks out to torment the nipple. It hardens and strains toward him like a sunflower to the heavens. He captures it with his mouth, his tongue laving the sensitive tip before he suckles. The ministrations of his mouth and tongue have found the secret wire that connects my nipple to my pleasure spot, that shuttles sensations from his hot wet tuggings straight to my sensitive core. With a pop, he releases it and treats my left breast to similar clever attentions.

"Ah, Adam. That feels ... so good." I growl the last word and he raises his eyes from the pillow of my breast and smiles. The sight of his grin unleashes a new flood of warmth between my legs, a juncture already drenched.

"I am deeply gratified that I please you, my love."

"You please me very much." I close my eyes and sigh.

The bed rocks. I open my eyes to find him looming over me. I close them again as his weight presses me into the downy softness of the mattress. A new perfume saturates the air of my bedroom, that of my own musky scent, the scent of arousal, the scent of invitation. Adam's olfactory workings should be processing these triggers. I await his next move.

"Shall I take you now, my love? Shall I slide into your velvety depths and savor your delicious wet tightness about my cock?"

"Oh, merciful savior, yes!" My voice is strangled and hoarse. "I mean, yes, I would like you to do that, Adam. Gently at first, though."

"I shall enjoy pleasing you, Letty," he whispers in my ear.

My eyes fly open. When did I teach him my nickname? His pace of learning has accelerated with unsettling rapidity. I must have left his audio sensors on and my communication system engaged one day, and he simply overhead my sisters or Lyle. My alarm dissipates and I luxuriate in how wicked the familiarity sounds on his lips.

"I adore how you feel, my love." I opt not to use his name but an endearment to assess the impact.

"I adore how you feel too, Violet, my love." His hands continue to caress my breasts, my sides, my belly. They tiptoe to my sex and part my folds. "Your sex is a rainforest of delight, my angel." He nips my neck where it meets my shoulder and triggers another wave of warmth to my quim.

My eyes shutter and I moan, "Aye ... rainforest ... lots of rain falling."

"I like you this way, trembling under my touch, blooming like a flower in the afternoon sun." He nips the other side of my neck, then the breast below it. "Mmm."

My heart races a little faster with his every moan. "Adam, please fuck me now," I pant. "I cannot bear much more."

"As you command, my love." His voice rumbles against my breast before he surges up against my body, the hairs on his chest stroking my skin.

The tip of his cock, hot and heavy prods against my body, probing, seeking my center. I move to align us and when he's settled into the sweet spot, he pushes forward.

"Oh, Violet!" He pushes in further. "My Violet." His cock penetrates my depths and stretches me. "Violet, you are perfection, so warm and snug. We fit like a hand in a glove, but I must move within you, my love, I must."

His unexpected diction thrills me, but when he begins to grind his hips against mine, I shoo those thoughts away for later analysis. "Yes. Just like that, Adam." I draw my legs up and around his back and he responds by moving deeper still. "Easy thrusts at first then building in intensity."

He obliges, and like the well-oiled machine that he is, pumps his hips in a rocking motion, stroking my inner walls.

I throw my head back into my pillow and just feel. Feel his rhythm. Feel the friction of our bodies moving together and apart. His sensors trigger his own groans of pleasure.

I ride wave after wave of delight, approaching the shore. My body tenses in preparation for my release. Muscles coil tightly like the warming up of a symphony awaiting the conductor's baton for that first explosive note. I am his instrument; his quickening movements play me like the fingering of frets.

Close, so close.

And then he pulls out.

I whimper with frustration. What glitch made him compute that this would be what I'd want? I bite my lip trying to hold back my scream of irritation at his ill-timed malfunction.

My consternation is short-lived because he's in motion again. He rolls to his back and takes me with him. With a wicked grin I've no idea where he found, he raises me by my waist, aligns the head of his cock with my opening, and then drops me. I gasp at his abrupt intrusion. He throws his head back and laughs, yes, laughs, another action I have not knowingly taught him.

His laughter dies and he refocuses on me, eyes locked with mine. And then he begins to move again.

He raises me and presses his own hips down before he drops me and surges up simultaneously. The impact nearly winds me; he is so deeply impaled in my body.

"Move for me, Violet."

I do. I dance my hips within the cradle of his, my legs on either side of his supine form. When I lean forward to vary the angle of his organ against my nubbin of pleasure, he seizes a nipple in his mouth and suckles. Hands that had previously guided my hips in their up and down motions, move to caress my thighs, his fingers alternately splaying and clenching.

I accelerate my movements, squeezing, tightening and bouncing on the plateau of his body.

He's so hard inside me, so hot, and I grip him with the possessiveness of a jealous lover. My muscles one by one relay a message of impending bliss. The tension grows and builds again.

"Yes, Violet. Ride me, my love. Ride me hard. Wrest your pleasure from me."

I squeeze my eyes shut and listen to him urge me onward, to ride him, up and down, back and forth.

I stop and, keeping as much of his blessed fullness inside me as possible, reverse my position.

"Lean back. I've got you," he whispers and he does. His hips rise and he thrusts into me from below.

"Oh..." I cry, but my voice shakes, a staccato as his pumping grows more ferocious. I crane my neck to look to the place where we join and marvel at the glistening sheen that encases his driving member. I drop my hand down to feel his point of entry, to touch the skin that wears my slick lubrication, far superior to any oil that courses through Adam's inner workings.

"Do I please you, my love?" His voice is gravelly and strained, like he's forcing his words out from behind clenched teeth. And still his cock moves within me.

"Yes, Adam. You please me very much." I can barely get my own words out because all my energy, my being, my senses are marching to where he is coaxing my nervous system into burnout.

Higher and higher I rise. His hands hold me firmly as he drives, and drives, and drives himself into me.

The cliff's edge looms then spins closer in a dizzying rush. Adam delivers a final shove and I fall over the edge. My insides somersault as I plummet into a chasm with no bottom. An unrestrained cry of completion pierces the room and I float in for a landing. I've no servants present to hear the evidence of my rapture, not tonight.

That's when I realize that Adam is still thrusting.

"Almost," he grits out before he suddenly stops with a long, loud groan. I catch myself from falling backwards because his grip on me has gone slack.

I rise up off his cock, still rock hard, and turn to inspect him.

His eyes have rolled back into their sockets; his mouth is frozen into a macabre grin that borders on a grimace.

"Adam?" I pat his cheek. "Adam?" I seize him by the jaw and turn his head from side to side. I'm almost ready to flip open his circuitry panel to check for a blown fuse when he suddenly blips back into consciousness.

"Yes, my love?"

"Just making sure you were still functional."

"Simply discharging my static electricity stores." He draws me in close and wraps his arms around me.

"What are you doing now, Adam?" I ask, somewhat puzzled by his post-coital tenderness. I add this to his growing list of non-organic intelligence markers.

"Cuddling, my love. Would you prefer that I initiate another round of intercourse instead?"

I nestle in close and sigh. I have done well. "Cuddling is good ... for now."

THE SUCCUBUS CHRONICLES

Chapter Four

I dream of Lyle. He comes to me as I lie in my bed and sits on the edge watching me. "I will always come when you call for me, my dearest heart."

His presence does not alarm me. "Kiss me." I reach my arms up to grasp him by his jacket fronts and pull him down to me.

He offers no resistance but shifts easily into my arms, lying atop me with only the thin coverlet separating us. Lips descend slowly to sip and taste mine, the softest brush to ignite my need further.

"More," I whisper against his lips.

With a groan, he kisses me again, parting my lips with his. His tongue slides against mine, does not invade but tantalizes. Our breaths mingle, steaming in and out through our noses as the kiss deepens. His groans answer mine and I am on fire.

"I don't want to hurt you, Letty," he says shifting his lips to my jaw. There he nips then licks his bites with his tongue before inching closer to my neck. "But devil take me, I want you so much, I ache."

My hips rock and undulate beneath his—coaxing, inviting, begging. "You can't hurt me in my dreams."

He lifts his head to peer into my eyes—his sorrow is painted in thick, ugly brushstrokes across his face—and then he is gone.

I wake to a pair of deep green eyes staring at me. "Adam?"

A grin blooms on his handsome face. "Adam? Is that what you named him? How biblical of you, Violet." He straightens and roars with laughter.

On the bed, behind my back, a body stirs to life. I roll over and squeak at the twin of the man I've just woken to. "Adam?"

"Yes, my love," says the male lying next to me.

"Oh, my God!" I sit bolt upright and cover my breasts with the sheets. Now that the sleep scales have fallen from my eyes and my brain, I understand my situation. "Lyle! How did you get in here?"

"Never mind that, you clever girl. What the deuce have you been making?" A few strides of his long legs carry him to the other side of the bed where Adam lies. "Adam? Is that your name?"

Adam sits and turns to me. "Who is this man, Violet, my dearest?"

Lyle's eyes grow wider. "Good Lord, he sounds exactly like ... me!" He reaches out a hand and pokes Adam in the cheek. "Not nearly as good-looking though."

"I am not a lord," Adam tells Lyle gravely, and I can't help but snicker at the shocked expression on Lyle's face. "I belong to Violet. By what name shall I address you?"

"You may call me ... Lord Cocksucker," Lyle says mocking my creation.

Adam laughs, sounding so like the man he was modeled after. "Lord Cocksucker. That is an interesting name. I like to have my cock sucked. Do you?"

Lyle sits on the bed next to Adam. "Oh, yes I do, very much. You're quite a lucky man if Violet sucks your cock. Does she?"

"Sometimes. Today I fucked her. It was our first time to have sexual intercourse, and I liked it very much. Violet is all any man could ever want in a lover."

"Yes, I dare say she would be. Lucky you, my friend."

"Lyle!" Both Lyle and Adam face me, one a pale replica of the other. "Adam, go to sleep now, please."

"As you wish." Adam lies supine and closes his eyes.

Lyle's eyes drift to the tent Adam's erect penis has created beneath the sheet. He reaches out and wraps a hand around the center pole. "A crude copy but nowhere near as grand as the real thing. Still, I applaud your taste." He casts a smirk my way. "However, I'm really wondering but one thought at this moment and that's … why?"

"Why?" I blink and wonder how much I should tell him. Given the extent of what he has discovered, I suppose no further harm can be dealt by sharing the why of Adam.

"Yes, why an inferior copy when you could have the superior original at the snap of your fingers?"

"Adam doesn't drain me. He recharges me. Therein lies the critical difference. Adam gives me what I need with the utmost discretion. Adam—"

"Is not me," he offers with a hint of wistfulness in his voice.

I have to break eye contact, can't have him seeing the regret I feel over the truth in his words. In a perfect world, I would have Lyle and I *would* love him, because a part of my heart has always yearned for him—his easy wit, his engaging discourses and his appreciation of my intellect and abilities other than those my anatomy provide. In that utopia I would finally fill the void in me, and not just the one between my legs. But I cannot reveal that to him, and instead I say what must be said. "No. He is not you."

Long, agonizing seconds tick by and neither of us speaks. Lyle finally rises. I don't watch him, but I hear him walk to the door, unlock it and leave. The telltale ticking of Adam's inner workings slow and then halt.

I drop my head into my hands. What have I done, making Adam as close a copy of Lyle as my artistic abilities could accomplish? Why have I not realized this sooner? Maybe if Lyle had stayed away like I had asked... Even if I change Adam's face, the voice is pure Lyle and that will always be enough to keep him fresh in my heart.

Suddenly the door bursts open, halting my recriminations. "Lyle!"

He rushes to my side and sits next to me. Taking my hand, he gazes at me, his energy crackling and electrifying the air around us. "You said Adam recharges you."

"Yes. That is his primary purpose."

"Would he recharge you enough to recover from me?" Wild green eyes entreat and seek to instill understanding, begging for...

My jaw and the penny drop in tandem. I scramble out of the bed, not even bothering to don a robe, and rush into my laboratory. I grab two bricks of coal and several of my tools. "If I can set Adam to function with greater intensity—greater force, speed, more simultaneous motions--maybe he can—oh, let's just see first."

"Yes, yes! Exactly what I was thinking and hoping. Adam satiates you beyond your needs and I take the rest." Lyle hands me my robe. "May I assist you? I've always had a fondness for steam and clockwork powered machines, and your skill with this automaton is absolutely amazing!" He moves to Adam's side of the bed and pulls back the sheet.

My pride swells at his words of praise. I didn't think I would ever be able to share my achievement with anyone, let alone the incubus—no, the man—who inspired him.

"Let me refuel him first. That needs a little time to get going." I scurry over to the coal burning stove heating my laboratory and extract a few glowing coals with my tongs. "These will serve as starters. Add two fresh coal briquettes to sustain him. Could you hand me that jug, please? I need to top off his water reserves, then I'll just need to tweak a few gauges that regulate the flow of the steam powering to his gears."

The panel in Adam's side easily slides open with slight pressure from my fingertips. "Hand me those needle-nosed pliers and hold the lantern overhead so I can see better, please."

Lyle does all as I ask and even anticipates other needs. He crowds in closer. A few screwdriver turns and another wire conduit added and Adam is clicking at an accelerated pace, his artificial heart pulsing with nearly the same excitement as mine. I glance up at Lyle who is grinning broadly, the shadows from the lantern dancing over his face and chest.

"Ready?"

"May I watch first?" he asks.

"Yes. Please. Once he's in pleasure mode, he won't respond to your voice, only mine."

"Even though he shares it?" He is teasing me but I'm too keyed up to pay him any heed, and in truth, I find the notion quite exciting.

"Adam?" I touch my creation on his sensory activation panel.

Adam's eyes flicker open and when he sees me, he smiles. "Yes, Violet."

"Good morning, Adam. Did you sleep well?"

"I did, thank you." He sits up and glances from me to Lyle. "Lord Cocksucker! Always a pleasure to see you again." Shifting his attention back to me he whispers, "Have you made another Adam, Violet?"

A giggle rises up within me, but I suppress it. "No, this man is your prototype."

Adam's handsome visage puckers as if in thought. He nods his head knowingly. "I see."

I give Lyle a wink before continuing. "Let's test a few of your motor functions, shall we? Adam, raise your right leg."

As if flinching from a red-hot poker, his right leg shoots up. Lyle barely avoids its treacherous path.

"Try again, Adam, only a little slower this time."

He does exactly as I ask. We go through a lengthy list of other motor skills that enable me to recalibrate Adam's responses to my desired levels of enthusiasm.

When I think he is finally ready, I fix Lyle with my stare and remove my robe. His darkened eyes and appreciative perusal of my body gratify me. A filament of understanding passes between us as well as an overwhelming wave of lust and need.

I am entrusting my well-being to a potent, virile incubus and a machine running at levels beyond the capacity of the gauges I've installed. I will adjust those later. So much can go wrong. Lyle might drain me. Adam might crush me. I press my lips firmly together and think instead of what *will* go right.

I lie down next to Adam. "Adam. I am desirous of your copulatory skills."

He turns his head and regards me with the most devilish smile, again surprising me with his quick ability to synthesize my responses and predict new ones. "Yes, my love." He snaps into a side lying position and whispers a finger from my forehead, down over my nose and lips, down my throat and into the valley between my breasts. He replaces his finger with his mouth, pressing light kisses in the same path before returning to my lips.

I moan and kiss him, too, opening my lips to receive his tongue and sliding mine against it. As we kiss, his fingers tiptoe to my sex to fondle and explore, moving me to the limit of what I can bear without being more thoroughly penetrated.

Adam changes the angle of his head as he repositions himself on top of me. He's heavy, but when I open my thighs, the pressure shifts from my chest to my hips. "You are so beautiful, my love," he whispers. Those lips move to my neck where his tongue swirls against my skin in the heat from his mouth.

"Yes, Adam, I like that," I say, my voice husky with need.

He supports more of his weight on his elbows. His hands move, his left threading through my hair to cradle my skull while the right skims over my breasts to my hips to my thighs. He pulls one leg higher. I wrap both around his narrow hips, pressing his rigid cock between us and moving against him.

Two new hands touch my legs and my eyes fly open. "Lyle!"

"Shh-shh-shh. Just trust me," Lyle says. He rubs his hands along my calves and to my insteps, repeating the soothing caresses again and again.

Adam takes both my wrists in one hand and pins them over my head. He moves off and lies on his side next to me. His mouth latches on to a nipple where he sucks, his hot tongue bathing it in warmth. He hums and groans, tugging gently with his lips and offering the occasional scrape of his teeth.

Lyle moves his head in between my splayed legs. His breath fans my sex. His fingers grip and push my thighs to open me further to him.

My back arches up and I cry out when Lyle's tongue plows a broad stroke between my folds then encircles but never touches my prime pleasure point. Adam ceases his suckling to smother my cries with a kiss. Lyle's ministrations continue to torment me. I reach a hand down to push his head away, saying, "Stop! I'll come, but it's too soon."

But he doesn't. If anything, his mouth grows hungrier, his tongue more cruel as it dives deep inside my channel, always skipping past the neediest part of my sex. Adam, too, is busy applying that marvelous mouth to my breasts, my neck, my ears and my lips.

"Adam," I can barely get the words out between gasps and kisses. "Watch Lyle, watch and learn."

"Yes, my love. Is what he is doing pleasurable to you?"

"Oh, Lord, yes!" I cry out as again, Lyle's tongue merely grazes my most aching parts.

"Then I will observe Lord Cocksucker as you wish." He releases my wrists and shifts farther down the bed, but his hands never stop touching me.

I glance down at the two dark heads—one buried between my legs, its tongue greedily lapping my lover's dew, the other resting on my mound of Venus, observing.

Lyle stops and pulls back. I catch his lust-glazed eye as he peers up at me. "Violet. Tell Adam to fuck you. Now!"

"Adam, I need—"

"I know what you need," Adam growls and quickly scrambles back between my legs. He positions the engorged head of his cock at my entrance and drives forward, stretching and filling me. He pulls back and surges forward again, moving even deeper.

"Merciful heavens, yes!" I shriek.

As Adam settles into a slow, gentle rhythm, Lyle rises up on his knees and strips off his shirt, exposing powerful broad shoulders and a lean but heavily muscled chest and stomach. His skin is sun-kissed, darker than Adam's, and covered in fine dusky hairs that have collected over his pectoral muscles before joining in the middle to form a path leading below the waistband of his breeches. The bed shakes as he jumps off to remove the last of his clothing.

He moves to the head of the bed and pulls my head to his cock, which rises up tall and proud from a thatch of ebony hair. I take his member into my mouth reaching for his sac beneath to give the soft balls inside a gentle squeeze. Lyle throws his head back and groans as I suck his cock and fondle his sac. I take as much of his length inside my mouth as I can, and when he hits the back of my throat, I arch my neck to grant him further passage. Adam kisses the pulse point beneath my ear, whispering all the endearments I taught him.

"Oh, Violet," Lyle grits out. His hips rock. He fucks my mouth with his cock while Adam does the same to my quim.

Lyle pulls out, muttering something about not wanting to come yet and that he can't believe how close he is. I know what I need to do.

"Faster and harder, Adam. Make me come." I capture Adam's mouth with mine and push my tongue against his, fucking his mouth with the same speed and aggressiveness as I'm demanding from his cock. He understands and matches the rhythm, hips pumping his cock deep inside me, ruthlessly plundering my depths. Our bodies slap together with increasing force and I think I'm going to tear apart, he's so large and aggressive in his mating.

"Violet, take him from above, if you need a respite." Lyle brushes the hair off my face and kisses my forehead.

"Adam, stop!" I bark. He does, without even a second's hesitation. "Get off me and lie on your back." He murmurs a few words of acquiescence and does that, too, helping me move into position atop him, like the magnificent stallion he is.

"Ride his cock, Violet," Lyle says, moving behind me. "Take his cock deep inside your pussy. I wish it were me fucking you. God knows, I wish it were me."

Adam reaches between his legs and holds himself steady for me. I position myself over his organ and fall down his full length, I'm so slick with excitement. When I bottom out, I can only groan.

Lyle touches and rubs my shoulders and my back. He holds me by the ass and moves me up and down Adam's length. "You like that, sweetheart? You like riding that machine you made?"

"Yes!" I cry from between gritted teeth. My voice shakes from my bouncing on top of Adam, who is whimpering and chattering a series of 'yes, yes, yes's' beneath me.

"Lean forward," Lyle says. He pushes me in that direction and a hand skates over the right globe of my ass. A finger squeezes in with Adam's cock inside my cunny. "You're so wet, Violet," he says withdrawing the finger to press it against sensitive nerves of my rectum. "Shall I take you this way? Fuck your ass while a machine does the honors to your cunt?"

I can't answer him. I'm too close to coming around Adam's cock. My muscles are tightening from the nearly unbearable tension building inside. Flutters in my belly, lightheadedness, all the signs of my imminent release are lining up to knock me off the cliff into the chasm below.

It's the slow push of Lyle's cock up my ass while Adam slams into my cunny from below that sends me hurtling into oblivion. I am falling and flying, falling and flying, and in the distance, beyond the rhythmic whooshing of my own pounding pulse in my ears, both Lyle and Adam are grunting rhythmically as they rut into me.

With a shout, Lyle surges forward one last time and stills as he spends, panting with each surge of his ejaculation. I wait for the telltale weakness Lyle is draining me to kick in, but it never comes. Instead, he grunts again and thrusts into me a few more times, giving a long extended groan as he finishes taking what he needs. I give Adam a tap on his shoulder to trigger his completion routine. He strokes into me one, two, three more times before roaring in a mockery of an orgasm.

"You were exquisite, my love," both men say in identical voices and in perfect unison, as if they'd read from a common script.

Lyle falls to the side and I wedge into the space between him and Adam.

When our breathing finally evens out, well, Lyle's and mine, Lyle brings my hand to his lips for a courtly kiss. "How do you feel, my love?"

"Like I could take on a pugilist and win and then ride cross country bare-back before traipsing up and down the stairs three at a time." I chuckle with happiness.

"Excellent. What sort of brilliant machinery shall we fashion next?"

"We?"

"Oh, yes. We. After I take you and Adam for a ride in my airship this afternoon, might I be so bold as to suggest that we make an Eve as a companion for your Adam?"

I roll my head to side to see how Adam is faring, hoping we haven't blown all his gears out of alignment.

"Adam, how are you—"

Before I can even finish, he nods and flashes me a huge grin before closing his eyes to enter stasis and cool down.

Pondering the wild notion of a threesome and even a foursome, I sigh and close my eyes, too, saying, "I think we're going to need a bigger bed."

"Anything you want, heart of my heart, anything at all."

The End

www.lilashaw.com

Evernight Publishing

www.evernightpublishing.com

www.ingramcontent.com/pod-product-compliance
Lightning Source LLC
Chambersburg PA
CBHW032156190626
46808CB00021B/1215